# Free Fall

## By S.D. Tuck

This book is a work of fiction. Names, characters, places, and incidents either are the products of the author's imagination or used fictitiously. Any resemblance to actual events or locales or persons, living or dead, is entirely coincidental.

All rights reserved

Copyright 2013 by S. D. Tuck.

This book is dedicated to
my husband Jim,
and to
Steve Olivas.

Chance stood on the rail of the bridge and looked down at the tarnished pewter-colored water below him. It looked unwelcoming, and unloved by the morning's first light. He knew at this moment that his thirty four years of living had always been leading him to this moment. He had no doubts and no hope; only regrets. The cold grey water mirrored his iron despair. He balanced easily on the edge of the railing. He noticed the metal around him was dew-pearled.

He had left his car at the entrance to the reddish metal bridge and walked to the midpoint. He thought of his wife. Missed her, as he had missed her these last twelve months. He felt his life was not so much unfinished, but more a life undone.

And so he stepped out of his insupportable present into the unsupported air, and fell feet-first to the cold wet mirror below.

Chance watched the dust cloud as it betrayed the track of the old Chevy pickup, as his Dad disappeared out of sight. He knew in his bones it was the last trace he would ever see of him. His stepmother was in the kitchen, weeping silent and red-eyed, only a little bit bruised. The red hens were still crouching under the hydrangea bush in the front yard, hiding from the tornadic rage that had just blown by. Chance had, as usual, been invisible to his father, who never thought to say good-bye as he drove out of his fourteen year old son's life.

Chance went around the back of the house to the pond and cast a line, fishing mostly for a moment of strength and some sense of belonging. He didn't want to go and comfort Lydia; he wanted to be comforted himself. Bayou, the old mutley farm dog, sidled up and pressed against Chance's knee. Chance rubbed his ears and looked down into the dog's brown eyes.

"Well, what do you think?"

Bayou answered by dropping open his mouth and panting his canine smile, looking hopefully at this boy he loved, hoping to ease his sorrow.

The ducks on the pond had paddled to the brink of the shore, quacking and gabbling, because Lydia was walking towards Chance and the pond. The ducks were ever hopeful of a handout. Chance looked with envy at the duck house, floating snugly on a tethered platform; a safe haven, removed from the reaches of the violent and voracious.

Lydia sat down on a log next to Chance, drying her hands on her dress.

"I guess he's gone this time."

"Could be." said Chance, noncommittally.

"He's done me so bad; I don't know what to do." She tried to stifle tears. "He's a mighty mean man."

"I reckon."

She tried to lean against him, he edged away. Lydia was a boney woman with a skillet face. She was forty, but life had knocked her hard and she looked aged beyond her years. She was desperate now for kindness, but Chance was afraid to give her much. It felt like she was climbing up on his back, trying to drown him.

Already at this young age, Chance knew about people grabbing what they could get a hold of in life, and then squeezing out whatever they could squeeze. They didn't really mean to squeeze all the juice out of people around them; they were just so thirsty they were blind to the harm they did to others. But, he didn't want to have any more squeezed out of him just then.

Lydia said, "Dinner's almost ready. I made pork chops and mashed potatoes, but your dad threw the pot of potatoes against the wall. The chops are still good, though." She was wheedling, tempting in her own mind.

"I need to go check the water tank for the Millers' cows. It probably needs topped up in this heat." It didn't, but he wanted to be somewhere else, away from her and her pain and her need.

"Your father took his truck. I'll drive you over in my car."

"No, don't bother; I'm going to ride my bike."

"But Chance!" she wailed.

He rode away, Bayou jogging by his side. He didn't look back either, no more than his father had. He rolled along the country lanes, turning down whatever road was shady, Bayou bouncing in and out of the streams as they crossed them; cooling his feet and slurping up water. Chance found his mind clearing and a sweet sense of freedom welled up in him. He didn't know where he was going and didn't really care. Just free in the rushing air, with his young legs pumping and his young lungs breathing deep and easy. Happiness flooded in.

He stopped at a river and took a swim to cool off. As he floated fully clothed, he looked up at the bridge where his bicycle was parked, and saw a little girl looking down at him.

"That your dog?" she asked, nodding at Bayou who was lounging in the shallows snapping at flies.

"Yes, it is."

"Can I pet him?"

"Sure."

The little girl whistled two notes and Bayou leapt up, ran up the embankment and wagged his way to her, eyes smiling, tongue lolling.

"Mecm wants to see you!" she shouted down to Chance. He got out of the water and climbed up to the girl and dog.

"Mimi said to bring you back home with me."

Alright." said Chance, wondering how Mimi knew he was there.

He wheeled his bicycle alongside the little girl and they walked down the shaded lane, the little girl keeping her hand on Bayou's head the entire time. The dog matched his step to that of the child, so they moved easily together.

Around the bend stood a small white house, back from the road. The front yard was filled with a blooming garden. And large old oaks sheltered the house from the heating sun. A porch ran all the way around the house. The porch swing looked inviting.

"Meem! Meem! Here we are!" the little girl jogged up the steps and opened the screen door. Inside was cool and shadowy. In the kitchen stood an older woman, greying curls, laughing face.

"Hello." said Chance, friendly but uncertain.

"Hello." said the woman, "I'm Grace." and she put out a hand to him. "I'm Marina's grandmother."

"I'm Chance, glad to meet you."

"Would you like to change out of those wet clothes? Here, have a glass of ice tea first. Do you take it sweet?"

"No, unsweet will be fine."

She had two glasses of tea, ready on the table, and handed them to Chance and Marina. Chance drank his down.

"Gracious! Would you like some more?" Grace was moving toward the old forty's-style refrigerator.

"No thank you, Miz Grace."

"Marina darling, take Chance upstairs and look in the hall closet. Some of your grandfather's clothes are still in there. Chance, you wear anything in there that suits you."

Marina and Chance went upstairs while Grace took a bowl of water to Bayou, on the porch. In the upstairs closet Chance found a cotton work shirt and some blue jeans that fit him well enough. He changed his clothes in a bathroom that hadn't changed in fifty years. In this house, it felt like he had stepped back in time. Everything was so old, but beautifully kept and cared for. He whistled a little as he buttoned his shirt.

When he got back downstairs, Grace had set out a plate with deviled eggs and some tomato slices, red and juicy, still sun warmed from the garden. She set a bowl of coleslaw next to it. She took off her apron. She was a slender woman, sprightly and trim.

"I know you're hungry!" she said to Chance, as she gestured to a place setting. The three of them sat down. Marina rocked a little in her chair, waiting impatiently for the guest to be served.

"Help yourself," said Grace. Chance was so hungry he had to remind himself to eat slowly and use his best, but rusty manners. Grace seemed to understand. Something about her made him feel comfortable and at home.

Chance told her that he had left home that day, and that no one was going to be looking for him to come back. She nodded easily, asked a few quiet questions, listened to him, gentle and impassive.

"Would you like to stay here a few days?" she asked him. "There are some things we could use a hand with— mowing for instance, and a few repairs on the barn."

"Yes ma'am, I would." said Chance and he smiled. He was flooded with a warm and unfamiliar feeling.


"Anybody home?" A man's voice called through the back screen door.

"Sure Buddy! Come on in." Grace said in a raised welcoming voice.

"Well who's this handsome stranger?" asked the man as he came into the kitchen.

"Buddy, this is Chance, a new friend we found down in the river. He's going to stay a few days and lend us a hand around here."

"Well good." answered Buddy. A man about Grace's age: lean and hard, showing a lot of mileage around the corners of his eyes and his thin mouth. His chin jutted out, firm. Chance hoped they were going to get along because Buddy didn't look like someone he wanted to tangle with. They shook hands. Buddy's hand was so round and strong, it felt like a live animal in Chance's hand.

Buddy helped himself to iced tea, asked Chance a few questions about where he came from, and then went out to work on the tractor.

"Chance, want to come along and keep me company?"

It was early evening, cooling now. Chance leaned against the tractor fender watching Buddy. He passed him a wrench when he asked for it.

"Grace is a lovely person. She's a kind and generous woman. If you do anything that hurts or upsets her, you will have to deal with me." He paused. "And I'll find you."

He dropped his eyes back to his work. Chance stood silent, then handed Buddy a screw driver, seeing he was about to need it. Marina came around back with Bayou, both charmed with the other's company. Buddy picked the child up and tossed her in the air. Marina laughed, Buddy was smiling openly. He set her down and she came and took Chance's hand.

At supper that night Marina announced, "I heard Buddy tell a lie."

"Really!" exclaimed Grace. Buddy stopped his fork halfway to his mouth.

"Yes," said Marina, "At the shop yesterday, when he was fixing Mr. Green's car. Mr. Green asked Buddy if he'd seen Mr. Green's donkeys, and Buddy said "no". But we HAD seen Mr. Green's donkeys. We saw them crossing the river early in the morning, when Buddy and me were driving to the shop. Isn't Buddy naughty to tell a big lie like that!" She settled back complacently in her chair, glad to be delivered of her news.

Buddy said, "Marina, if it's raining out and you stand on the porch, are your feet wet or dry?"

"Dry." said Marina.

"And if you go out in the yard in the rain and stomp in puddles, are your feet wet or dry?"

"Wet!" squealed Marina happily.

"Now, if you stand on the edge of the ocean, and some waves are washing around your feet and some waves don't reach that far, are you standing in the water or not?"

Marina looked at him doubtfully.

"If I know Mr. Green starves those donkeys, beats them, and is working them to death, is it right for me to tell him where they've gone, when they run away?"

"It's better not to tell him." Marina answered instantly. "But," she said after a pause, "It's still a lie."

"It's not always simple to do what is right. You can be stupid-honest or you can be wise."

Well how do I know?" asked Marina.

"You have to think."

Grace reached out across the table and took Marina's hand. "Darlin, when someone who does bad things asks you questions, you don't have to tell them what you know. You want to protect the innocent from the cruel if you can. Rules are important, but don't ever follow them blindly. Always use your good sense!"

"Or," laughed Buddy, "stay on the porch your whole life, and never get your feet wet!"

Grace and Marina laughed but Chance said, "Sometimes you don't have a porch to get up on."

That silenced the laughter. Grace reached across the table and this time took Chance's hand. "Well you've got a porch from now on." Then she let go of his hand and said, "Who wants pie?"

Grace made up a bed on the screened-in porch and Chance fell asleep to the night sounds of the woods and fields.

In the morning, Grace drove into town to an aqua class at the county recreation center. Dancing around in the water made her feel young and easy. The indoor pool was always packed full of women from the town and the countryside. Also a few old men with surgry scars like crucifixes on their chests. Some of the women were as round as they were tall. Grace thought they looked like a group of large pretty beach balls bobbing up and down. The instructor stood on the pool deck and hollered instructions that were muffled by the echoing noise from the tiles and roof. She had the bobbing people doing jacks and skiing under the water, jumping imaginary barrels, and marching like soldiers. The water churned and splashed as if a school of fish were in a frenzy below the surface. Most of the people in the class had terrible health problems, or had been through hell and back on a surgical gurney. You wouldn't know it to look at them or listen to them. They sounded like the Millertown Garden Club, and in fact a number of them were. Their gentile way of talking that occasionally lapsed into simpering, was strangely at odds with their large crinkle-clad floating roundness. Like seals in plum or black colored bathing suits, thought Grace.

Although their words sounded honeyed, there were plenty of spikes dripping there. Grace overheard "Did you see what she was wearing for underwear? I wouldn't dress my dog in that!" and

"Miz Snooty Two Shoes over there has another new bathing suit, I see. Must be nice!"

"I heard Ruth, that school teacher there, sent Annie's youngest boy home last week for no good reason, said he looked like he had the Itch. Annie's going to the principle, she says she's tired of having her boy picked on by snobby town folk."

Grace's friend Emily whispered to her, "I thought cats didn't like water!" Grace giggled.

Because the pool was crowded, some people got pushed against the wall or into their neighbors. Occasionally, an elbow jabbed back at someone getting too close. One of the old men said to the woman bobbing in front of him, "If you had got any closer on that last step, I was gonna hug you."

Halfway through the hour, the instructor yelled, "Okay Ladies, grab your noodles."

People dashed to the poolsides and pulled in four-foot long white foam tubes, which they rode astride like rocking horses. They held little blue foam dumbbells in either hand, tipping off balance and chortling.

"Ladies, bicycle! Pump harder! Push harder! Travel across the pool. You on that half go toward the windows, and you other half go toward the hot tub. That's right, go towards each other!"

The thirty ladies kicked and heaved and paddled through each other, tipping and knocking clumsily. The woman coming towards Grace was waving her foam weight in the air, struggling to stay mounted. Grace fended her off, to avoid being whacked in the head. The woman yelped and fell off her noodle. The woman shouted as Grace passed, "You wet my hair, you ruined my hairdo!"

The woman's friend grabbed Grace's noodle and gave it a twist, trying to unseat her. Grace rode the attack off, laughing and waving her weights in the air, keeping her balance. Emily, using her soft foam weights, batted at Grace's foe. They boxed like kangaroos, knocking into the women around them. One woman yelled,

"Drown the Townies!"

Someone answered, "Tip the Trash!" The women were all hooting and laughing now, jousting like knights on noodle ponies. The teacher was shrill,

"Ladies! Ladies! Stop this now!"

The two young lifeguards jumped in to break it up and half the ladies turned on them, knocking them over and pummeling them with the harmless blue barbells. White noodles hurtled through the air. The director arrived, blowing his whistle frantically. By then, the ladies had tired themselves and were clutching the poolsides, exhausted with laughter and the first real exercise that some of them had had in years.

The following day, the Millertown hair-dressers were flooded with the wreck of blue rinse and waves on the heads of many of their older clientele.


Chance's few days with Grace stretched through the summer's end. In August she registered him for high school in town.

Bayou stayed three years, then left on a river of tears. They buried him beneath one of the old oaks in the side yard. Marina wept again as she planted red impatiens over his shallow bones.

The year following Bayou's departure was Chance's senior year at school. One night he was sitting on the front steps of the porch, Marina at his side. Buddy had his arm around Grace, as they slowly rocked in the porch swing.

"Mr. Taylor, my swimming coach, says I should think about joining the National Guard." said Chance. "He says it will make a man out of me. If I'm in the Guard, I'll get to see the world for free. If I decide to go to college after, they'd help out with that. What do you think, Buddy?"

Buddy replied, "I think Mr. Taylor is a well-intentioned fellow, but it sounds like he's saying, "There's a man in a car over there who will give you some candy, if you'll just ride with him." Once you swallow that candy, those doors are going to lock and there will be no turning back. They got you and the way things are going, they'll send you off to fight for God knows what. A man has to choose his own fights. When the right one comes, you'll know it and you can go right down that day and volunteer in the Army. Until then, you don't need to ride on the back of the U.S. Federal Government to become a man. If you'll just stand on your own two feet and look the world straight in the eye, biology is going to do the rest for you.

If you want to see the world, why not go work your way around it? You'll see the world! My advice to you is always paddle your own canoe, and let the Federal Government get along without you."

Chance decided to follow Buddy's advice. He worked at the garage that summer and worked weekends at the grocery store. He saved his money and in the fall headed off for New York City, in an old blue Chevy pickup truck that Buddy and Grace gave him to carry him on his way.

He drove all day, excited even by the dull miles of endless four-lane. After dark he wheeled into a gas station-café somewhere in West Virginia. He fueled up the gas tank and looked for a place to park. All the spaces in front of the café were taken, so he parked on the edge of the lot and walked back to the lighted building. He sat at the counter and ordered a cup of coffee from a rough-looking bleach blond-headed woman. As he sipped the tepid coffee, hours-old swill, he noticed two guys sitting in a booth eyeing him. He drained his cup, put two quarters on the counter and headed for the men's room. Out of the corner of his eye, he saw the waitress glance at the two men, then look at him and nod her head. He was sitting in the stall when he heard the men's room door open. Someone walked past the door of the stall and stood silent. The lights went out. Chance finished his business, hitched his pants and buckled his belt. Then he silently slid the bolt back on the stall door. In the total darkness, he suddenly and savagely kicked the stall door open, smashing the man who was standing there. Chance ran to the door of the room, hurled it open and saw the other man standing in the narrow dark hallway, blocking the doorway into the café. He looked to his left, saw an exit door, and ran.

"Thank God it's unlocked!" he thought as he whirled through it and out into the night. As he ran around the corner of the building towards the lights, he heard the man cursing as he pursued him. Chance decided not to run for his truck, it was too isolated out in the dark. There was a semi pulled up on the side of the café and Chance bounded up the passenger side. Again, an unlocked door. He slid inside, clicked the door shut and huddled, panting and shaking on the floorboards. He heard another click and felt something cold and hard press against the back of his head.

"What the hell do you want?" demanded a big voice. Chance started to turn around, but the man said,

"Hold it right there! I asked, what the hell do you want?"

"I'm running from two men who jumped me in the bathroom." Chance gasped.

"Oh really!" The man clicked on the cab light. "Turn around, let me look at you."

Chance was fighting back tears as he turned to face the pistol. The man holding it went back to lazing in the bunk behind the seats. He weighed at least 300 pounds, and his face loomed at Chance like a jowly dog. After he looked Chance over, he lowered his gun.

"What are you doing here at this place?" he asked.

"I was getting gas, I'm just traveling through."

"Well you picked a hell of a place to take a piss! Are you driving a blue pickup by any chance? Jack and Jasper are fixing to put a tire iron through the windshield."

"Oh God!" whispered Chance.

"Hold on." said the truck driver. He mountained into the driver's seat, rolled down the window and yelled, "Hey Jack, you out swatting flies in the dark? If you're thinking of changing a tire on my friend's truck, you'll find he keeps his tires right down there on the ground. He's funny that way." Then he laughed a deep stenourous wheeze.

"He's a friend of yours, Leo?" disbelief in the man's voice.

"He sure is, and I am not going to take it kindly if you make a mess of his truck."

Leo told Chance he could get up off the floor now. Chance sat in the passenger's seat and saw his two assailants going back into the café. Leo asked Chance where he was going and where he was from, then said,

"I'll tell you what, I've had enough hours off the road, I'm legal to drive some more. I'm going North, I'll just follow you up the highway a few hours, til you're out of range of these polecats. You picked some shark tank to take a piss in!" He laughed his raspy choking wheeze again, lit a cigarette, and drove his rig over to Chance's truck.

"You just drive as fast as you can." he told Chance as Chance climbed down. "I don't want to lose any more time than I have to."

Chance's hand was shaking so hard he had trouble getting the key in the ignition, but finally he cranked the engine and gave Leo what he hoped was a nonchalant nod. Together they convoyed out to the highway and rolled several weary hours into Maryland. After about one hundred miles more, Leo honked his clarion horn and powered on by, waving out the window as he was swallowed by the night.

Chance pulled into the first rest stop and parked under a bright light in front of a closed information booth. He locked his doors, made a pillow of his jacket, and fell into a restless sleep hunted by dreams.

The next day he drove the long corridor of northeastern turnpikes. Concrete barriers herded him into the tightly packed suburbs of New Jersey, where Grace's cousin's widow lived. He searched among miles of blocks of sameness houses: boxy, unloved, barely- tended. All yards chain-linked, all doorbells strident.

He felt a little ground down as he rang the bell. A woman's voice asked through the door, what he wanted.

"It's Chance St. Clair." he said, embarrassed. "Grace wrote to you."

"You don't look like Grace's grandson."

Chance noticed the peephole in the door. He tried to arrange his expression. "Well I can't help that!" he said, surprised that Grace had said he was her grandson.

Gertrude opened the door and he opened the glass storm door. She stood aside to let him in. Her hair was in curlers, and she was dressed in a lumpy chenille bathrobe and pink plush slippers that had tendered many a live cigarette dropping. From the smell of the room, the thick shag rug had done its share of smoking as well, over a lengthy lifetime. The television was on. A cigarette burned in an ashtray on the table in front of the slip-covered sofa.

"The guest room is upstairs on the right."

As Chance brought his backpack in, Gertrude frowned disapprovingly. He took it up the shag clad stairs and dropped it on to the bed in a square blank of a small room. The one window was half filled with an old air conditioner.

"It's time to eat!" Gertrude yelled up the stairwell. They ate TV dinners in the gloaming of the TV screen.

"So Grace's letter says you want to see New York?"

Chance nodded, not caring to shout above the evening news.

"I don't know why you want to go over there. We have everything we need right here on the Jersey side. Nothing but muggings and overpriced parking in the city. I haven't been across the river in years."

Chance looked at her in disbelief. "Well I think I'll have a little look since I've come this far."

"Suit yourself. Waste of time if you ask me. You probably better leave your truck here and take the bus in. Cost you thirty-forty dollars to park over there!"

In the morning, he and Gertrude each had a bowl of cereal and plenty of coffee, before she left for work. He asked where he could get on the bus to go into the city.

"Beats me!" Gertrude said, "But my neighbor has a nephew who goes in all the time."

She called her neighbor who said Brent was going in that afternoon and would take Chance with him. Brent turned out to be a lively, friendly young man, and Chance's spirits lifted as he left the harsh staleness of the house.

As they crossed the river, Chance saw the city for the first time. It seemed to him both ethereal and engineered, tightly bounded by the river, reaching slim and graceful to the sky. Brent was talking but Chance had ceased to listen.

"What do you want to do tonight?" Brent asked him.

"I don't know: see the Empire State Building, the Statue of Liberty?"

"Man, you're kidding, right?"

"No." said Chance uncertainly.

"Those are tourist places, that's way uncool. Let's take in the nightlife! Let's start uptown and work our way down."

From the Port Authority, they took a bus uptown. Chance was bewildered by the sheer mass of humanity, pushing against him, flowing around him. People were yelling, cabs honking, policemen blowing whistles, music pouring out of storefronts. On the bus, a very strange looking black man with wild hair walked the aisle waving his arms and talking loudly.

"Don't look at him." advised Brent. Chance immediately looked out the window. He watched the turmoil as the bus stopped and started and lurched uptown. He was captivated, the excited energy thrilled him. Brent pulled the chord and they stepped down to the curb. Brent steered him into a bar.

The door hushed closed behind them, and the din was silenced. A bartender stood polishing a glass with a white dishtowel, bottles gleaming sweetly on the shelf behind his head. One man sat drinking slowly at the bar. Brent ordered them both a draft, and slid into a cushioned booth. Chance leaned back letting the padded leather embrace him. He sipped his beer, feeling he had made it to a place in life where he wanted to be.

He and Brent talked and chaffed happily. Brent filled him in on young savvy. Chance was an eager learner.

They went back into the hot roaring savagery and walked south, commenting on the people they saw, looking in shop windows, and laughing at a gay couple having a lover's quarrel while entangled in the leashes of six baby Pekinese.

After a few blocks they turned into another bar. Music was playing, a pool table was busy, and there were a few more patrons, young men like themselves. They played a little pool, Chance coming away with twenty dollars and no hard feelings. He said it was a few lucky breaks.

The next place they stopped was a fern bar. More people, more music, more food. A couple of pretty girls were being lively on their bar stools. Chance bought them each a drink and the night started.

After dinner, the four of them agreed to walk down Sixth Avenue, stopping in every bar until they reached dawn. Katje, who was now Chance's girl, said she'd always wanted to see the flower market that flourished at the break of day, downtown on the Avenue of the Americas. Chance said he would show it to her.

So they walked and they drank and they danced. They laughed a lot. In the wee hours, they found themselves all crowded into a small bathroom, snorting a little bit of coke through a ten dollar bill. Friendliness grew and lines grew blurry. Arms around bodies, music was beating, kisses became passionate. Chance felt both sloppy beautiful and crystally enlightened, at the same time. It was bliss.

They did make their way to sunrise and the four of them watched the flower vendors set out an ocean of sweet smelling, color-singing flowers in the almost opening dawn.

Then Katje took Chance home to her third floor apartment and took the very young man to her bed. Because they were young and lithe, the night of drinking and sleeplessness had not tired them-it had exhilarated them. Their physical appetite for each other was deep. One wave ending was a new wave beginning. They slid and tangled through the early hours, slept a few hours, then rode, grasped and tumbled again.

Finally, satiated for the moment, they ravaged the findings of the kitchen, and then slept deeply in each other's arms.

In the evening, they chased the shadows of the night most of the way to daybreak again. They surged with passion through the small hours and slept into Sunday afternoon. Chance woke and looked at Katje sleeping. She had looked pretty when he met her; she was now beautiful to him. He felt himself drowning in gratitude, disabled. When she was awake, he tried to tell her tenderly.

"I never knew…... You took me somewhere. It was a night of magic! You are so beautiful. Thank you." he breathed, almost reverentially.

She laughed at him and said, "Lighten up, Babe, I didn't take you anywhere. I'm not a chauffeur, we went on that joy ride together."

He went back to Gertrude's that night, Katje had to work the next day. He returned to New Jersey a more educated man than when he left. Gertrude was in the living room, smoking her way through a dinner tray.

"Where the hell were you?"

"I was staying with a friend." he replied.

"Friend? You don't have any friends in New York! Brent dragged in here yesterday morning-had no idea where you were. Grace called this morning. I told her you hadn't come back in two nights. Why the hell didn't you call and say where the hell you were?"

"I guess I forgot." answered Chance. He had been swept up in a whirlwind and never gave a thought to New Jersey that weekend.

"You FORGOT? Well you can also forget about staying here if this is the way you are going to act."

Chance was unmoved by her anger, experience told him it carried no weight.

"I'm really sorry, it won't happen again."

You're damned right it won't!" She stubbed her cigarette out angrily. "If it weren't for Grace, your ass would be curbside right now!"

Chance managed to soothe her and she agreed he could stay a week or maybe two, until he found another place. He agreed to do some work on the house.

He called Grace. She was relieved to hear from him.

"I'm fine, just having a good time in the City."

"It doesn't seem like you to let Gertrude worry."

"Yeah, I know, sorry about that."

"Well, I was just surprised, that's all."

After he hung up, he stood with his hand still on the receiver, feeling the distance stretching greater between them. He felt no nostalgia-he loved them at home but all of his attention was on this bright new time. He felt strong and alive and free.

During the week, he fixed Gertrude's leaking kitchen sink, changed the blown light bulb over the front door, and cleaned the air conditioner filters. He also visited the Statue of Liberty and the Empire State Building, and wandered alone and happy-discovering Manhattan, but going back to Gertrude's in the evening. On Friday he told Gertrude he would be gone for the weekend and headed to Katje's apartment. Another weekend; same excitement.

It became a pattern. Gertrude was prepared to have Chance stay on as long as he continued to repair her neglected house. He was not tiring of the beat of the dance, the alcoholic splendor, or the physical tangle with Katje. They laughed and joked their way through part of the summer, he blended easily with her friends.

One weekend they took the train to a small town on the Connecticut coast. Her aunt, Marie, was driving a Mercedes when she picked them up at the station. When Chance got in, he recognized that even the smell inside the car was luxurious. It was his first proximity to casual wealth. Through the window, he saw large trim clapboard houses, graceful gardens and plenty of expensive cars. He glimpsed the Long Island Sound between the houses. The blueness startled him each time. The houses, the lawns, even the bright blue water spoke of privilege with such quiet assurance that Chance felt shrunken inside. When they turned into a driveway and parked next to a Jaguar convertible, he thought maybe he should not have come. His old pack and his soft southern accent seemed lost and disenfranchised.

Marie was pleasant and unapproachable. She was warm with Katje. Chance thought she was probably human.

"Just set your luggage down here," she said as they walked into the front hall. Chance could see straight through the dining room through the window, and across a green lawn to the water. He saw a thirty-five foot sailboat at the floating dock in front of the house. Katje's uncle was on board, opening a hatch.

"Looks like Uncle Mark is getting the Spinthrift ready to go out." commented Katje.

"Go if you want to." said Marie. Chance thought to himself, "Want to! Die for is more like." He could not believe how casual she was. He nudged Katje, who said,

"Oh yes, we would love to go for a sail."

"Go down and let him know."

They walked across the cushioned lawn and down the cleated boards of the ramp to the dock. Mark gave his niece a hug, genuinely glad to see her. He shook Chance's hand and said,

"We'll make a sailor of you, lad." He showed Chance how to cast off and coil the lines. Katje showed him how to hoist the jib as they eased off the dock into a cheerful breeze.

When they raised the mainsail, the boom and the canvas sounded the sharp cracking snap dear to every sailor's heart. Chance grinned as wide as ever he had. The three of them sailed the stout wooden sloop over the dimpled sea, with the wind in Chance's face and the spray slapping over him.

They came in an hour before sunset, before the afternoon wind dropped. Spinthrift was moored on her buoy and they stepped into the sprightly white dingy. Katye showed him how to fit the oarlocks into their holes and he rowed them back to the dock. Mark put an arm around Chance's shoulder as they walked toward the house. One sailor recognized another.

"I guess I don't need to make a sailor of you, you seem to have been born one."

Through dinner Chance asked and Mark answered: stories, details, neat little tricks in handling a boat, wood versus fiberglass. The two men sat up late drinking brandy.

The next morning was bright and sunny with a brisk wind. Katje decided to go shopping with Marie; but Mark and Chance went straight down to the Spinthrift, lunch in a hamper, determined to spend the day on the water.

Mark turned the helm over to Chance. The feel of the sea and the feel of the old wooden boat came up through his legs and through his hands. A sense of mastery and power that most men will never know was his in those moments.

They sailed all day. Chance was sorry when they headed for the dock. He and Katje took an evening train back to New York, but for once, the city was not his lodestar. He missed the last bus for New Jersey and stayed at Katje's that Sunday night. For the first time, he did not take her in his arms. Instead, after a day of sun and wind he fell asleep at once and rocked in his dreams on the water.

The next day as he took the bus across the river to New Jersey, he was lost in thought. He spent the week repairing more of Gertrude's neglect. On Friday afternoon, Mark called and suggested he come up for another weekend of sailing. Chance immediately agreed.

He called Katje from the train station and said he would not see her that weekend. It posed no problem to her. He was a friendly pleasure and she expected to have no regrets when they drifted off to other lovers.

The weekend was drizzily, but Chance spent a happy time varnishing trim, scouring decks, and tinkering with the diesel engine. On Sunday, Mark asked him if he would like a job as deckhand on the Spinthrift. There was a room above the garage that he could live in. The wages were modest, but weekends would be his. Chance took the afternoon train back to New Jersey, and said good-bye to Gertrude that night. He drove his old truck to Connecticut the following day, stopping only for gas and to buy an electric percolator and a hot plate.

His new home had a window looking out over the water, an old twin bed, cast off from the house a long time ago, and a tired linoleum floor. It looked like heaven to

Chance, as he watched the Spinthrift bobbing on her mooring in the moonlight.

Mark already had one boat-hand, Devon, who worked as crew on the weekends; but the wooden boat needed continual care, repair and refurbishing. Marie called it a hole in the water in which to throw money.

"I don't know why you won't get a fiberglass boat. All you have to do is sail them. Our friends just go out on their boats and sail. They don't spend all their time and money on upkeep and repairs. They just pop them out of the water for the winter, and pop them back in, in the summer. No leaking and swelling and caulking every single summer after the launch!"

"Yeah and if they ever get into really rough water, those glass hulls are going to fold up like paper, no stability or inner fortitude at all." said Mark defensively. "A glass boat has no heart, no tradition-just halyards slapping on a steel mast. Not for me, no thank you!"

Marie primmed her mouth and looked away.

Mark continued, "You never go out on the boat anyway, what do you care?"

"I just think it's antiquated. It looks like an old tub alongside the other boats."

Chance knew it didn't. The Spinthrift looked lean, elegant, smooth. It lifted his heart every time he looked at her lines. He was happy to spend most of his time caulking, painting, polishing brass. He spent weekends sailing with Mark and Devon, occasionally going down to see Katje.

Devon, from upstate New York, was a little older than Chance. He had crewed every summer and was a capable sailor. He chafed on Chance, riding a little high and hitting a little low. But Chance recognized his skill and his quickness. Sometimes they'd go out and have a beer and a game of darts. Devon didn't lose well, but Chance didn't play hard, so they got along well enough. Devon hit hard on the women: good looks and confidence assisted him.

Chance coasted easily, and that, too, worked well with the women around him.

In September Devon went home to continue pursuing an electrician's license at the local trade school. Chance stayed on with the Spinthrift, Mark didn't haul her until Thanksgiving. Often they were the only boat on the water. By now, Chance handled her fairly well. Mark was a consummate sailor. The boat took the autumn winds well, and they drove her rail under as the seas climbed. No greater happiness then when they coasted on the tense edge of blow-down.

Chance worked for Mark for two years, moonlighting in the boatyard sometimes in the winters. He spent some time in New York, and Katje came up for the weekend from time to time; but in the second summer she found love and set Chance loose. He was not bruised but it left a hole. He had some pals at the bar and at the boatyard. And he had a few light flirtations running, but Katje had been a warm shoulder and a willing lover. He would miss her wit, as well.

"So she dumped you, you wharf rat." Devon observed. He had envied Chance. Katje had been dismissively uninterested in Devon.

"Yeah, I guess so." was all Chance said.

"You'll get over it, but what a babe to let get away!"

Chance said nothing.

"Now I'll tell you who's a looker: that Marie puts her niece in the shade!"

"Isn't she a little old?" asked Chance.

"No way. Don't you know the fruit gets sweeter hanging on the tree." He smacked his lips.

Chance didn't agree, his mind flashing to Katje, moving naked in the night. "I wonder if Mark would want to hear you say that?"

"Oh Mark, he's all wrapped up in his boat and his work-he's an idiot."

"Chance said, "I don't think so. He's been mighty good to me."

"Oh yeah, letting you freeze in that little room in the winter, while he stretches out in front of his fire in his big house. You crackers stay dumb no matter how much salt you get on you."

"I beg your pardon."

"I said an old cracker is not a wise cracker, hee hee."

Chance hit him, caught him in the jaw and knocked him down.

"Man, what did you do that for?"

"I guess I'm too dumb to know any better."

Devon appeared to bear no ill-will, and began calling him Mr. Saltine, which rapidly degenerated to Salty.

In the fall, when Devon was leaving he said, "Hey, Old Salt, why don't you spend the winter in Upstate? You can stay with my brother and me. There's all kind of Christmas jobs-help you make the rent."

In a moment of weakness, Chance agreed. Mark was not pleased.

"Chance, the only reason I have Devon around is because he can crew my boat. He's not somebody to associate with. Why don't you stay here and take some courses at the community college? I know you can get a scholarship, and I'd be happy to let you keep on living here. If you wanted to start taking some finance and business courses, I'm sure I could work you into my firm somewhere. You could work your way up. You know Katje works for me and she seems to like it."

Chance knew that Katje was bored to death at work. She saw it merely as a means to live and play in the city life.

"That's mighty tempting," he said, "and I thank you; but I don't think that's going to be the right direction for me. I really do appreciate the opportunity."

"I'm disappointed in you, Chance. I think you're making a big mistake. You need to have better judgment about whom you choose for your associates."

"I'm sorry you feel that way. You're probably right, but it's my chance to see a new part of the country. I really want to do that."

"Well don't come crying to me." finished Mark, angry at seeing Chance throw away a golden offer.


Chance called Grace on Thanksgiving, shortly before he left for New York State.

"Chance, I'm so glad to hear from you. How have you been? We've been thinking about you."

The warmth of her affection and her dulcet southern tone sent wave after wave of sweetness through him.

"So tell me the news!" he said.

"I guess the big news is Marina won the science fair at her school, and then went on to win the state. She's going to Washington for the National High School Science Competition."

"What in the world was her project?"

"Well, you know how crazy she is about animals- she just about flunked biology because she wouldn't pith a frog."

"Yeah, I remember you telling me that." he laughed.

"So she's been saving tree frog eggs out of the rain barrel and letting them hatch in a kiddie pool. She did a project with the tadpoles, showing how different water temperatures, and various minerals and alkalinity affect their development. It's really complicated, and it turns out that frog specialists didn't know some of these things."

"I'm proud to know her." said Chance.

"I'll tell her you said that, it will mean a lot to her. Some of the judges at the state level wanted to keep the little baby frogs and dissect them. "

"Oh Lord, I can imagine Marina!" he said, laughing again, thinking of her earnest defiance when it came to protecting an animal.

"You would have thought they were her babies!" chortled Grace. "So anyhow, all the little froglets came home safe and sound. She let them go next to the kiddie pool."

Before they hung up, she said, "We miss you a lot. Buddy says to say "hi"."

He began to miss them, too. As he drove the snowy parkway, drifted beautiful and silent, he thought a lot about Grace and Buddy and Marina. He hoped life wasn't carrying him too far from them.

The little village where Devon lived was sunken in snow to its windows. Through the windshield it looked like a Christmas village in a model train set.

"Hey Old Salt! " shouted Devon, coming out of the door and crunching down the salted sidewalk. He punched Chance in the shoulder, a little too hard. "Thought you'd never get here-what took you?"

"Had a little snow in front of me." mentioned Chance.

"That slowed you down? Salty, you need a bigger set!"

Someone behind Devon cringed. "Devon, you are so crude!"

"This is Miss Manners, my sister." mocked Devon.

She reached around and put out a hand to Chance, saying, "Welcome. I'm Victoria. I've been curious to meet anyone callous enough to be a friend of Devon's."

"Old Saltine here isn't bright enough to know any better. Or at least that's what his fist mentioned to me."

"You grate." she said coldly. Devon grinned at her. She turned and glided trimly up the icy walk.

Chance had arrived at Devon's parents. Devon's mother had cooked a welcome pot roast. Chance was the first southern boy they had met and there were many questions that left Chance tired and lonely. At last he rose from the table and said,

"We have shoes, we have teeth, and we have manners. Now if you will excuse me, I've been traveling all day and I would like to go to sleep. Thank you."

The whole table laughed. He followed Devon and his brother, Jack, out through the door into the immense cold. He drove behind them, losing them sometimes as Devon fishtailed around corners. Soon enough, they pulled up in front of a closed café, climbed the stairs of a hallway next door, and Chance tumbled into a sprung spring bed, dropping his pack onto the floor and falling into an exhausted sleep.

That night he dreamt of Buddy and Grace, Marina and Bayou. It was a sweet dream of warmth remembered, and lasting love known.

That winter was snowbound. Chance worked at the hardware store for Gus and Judy. Gus was big, with a bushy grey beard. Judy was small and round with an apple pie smile. They too tried to warn Chance away from Devon.

"He's not the kind of young man a person wants around. Some of the girls in town are crazy about him, but he's been too free with some of them, and then just walked away. Nice girls-kind of girls don't usually get in that kind of trouble." Judy was sad as she said this.

Gus added, "And he's a bit too free with other people's property."

"Now Gus," chided Judy, "He's never actually been caught doing that!"

"Yeah, because he's a bit too clever by far. He never gets caught, but doesn't mind getting his friends into trouble. Poor John Burton got expelled when he and Devon were in high school. Somebody broke into the school and tore things up. Threw red paint around, made an awful mess. Devon whispered a word in the principle's ear, John Burton got expelled, but we all know Devon did it!"

"Gus, nobody knows that for sure." said Judy. "John had been in a little trouble before that, stealing gas and all!"

"Well I'm sure!" finished Gus emphatically. Chance took it under advisement, but continued to live with Devon and his brother. They spent evenings drinking beer and shooting darts. Devon was very funny and sharp, edgy good company. The three young men spent some nights skating in the dark on the frozen river, racing for miles in the icy cold. Devon's sister, Victoria began to join them on these outings. It was exciting and risky, speed gliding following the clear channel of ice, where the wind had blown the snow away. They jumped logs, clipped snow banks, fell hard and slid far. One night Jack was in the lead and fell through thin ice. Devon lay down across the thinning ice, while Chance squatted on the thicker ice, and held Devon's ankles. Together they hauled Jack out of the icy dark water. His lips were blue. Chance gave him his dry jacket and the four of them skated home fast, making Jack move fast and hard to keep him from freezing. Devon mocked, "Nice going, sport."

Some nights the three boys ate dinner with Devon's parents. Victoria lived at home as did the youngest child, Danny, who was eight. Victoria was studying to be a paralegal, at the community college.

One night Chance asked her if she would go out with him.

"Where were you thinking of taking me?" she asked.

"I don't know. Where would you like to go?"

"How about the Royal Coach Inn?"

Chance gulped. He said slowly, "We-ell, I don't have a jacket or dress shirt."

"Then I guess I'll go out with you when you do." she said snippily.

Devon overheard her and said, "You're going to need some ice-fishing gear if you're going to date Vicky. Maybe Gus will give you a discount. Get a hand-warmer, too. You'll need it!" He laughed small. Victoria got up and walked away.

Chance bought a jacket that week and on Saturday night took her to the inn. She ordered wine and lobster. He swallowed hard, and then did the same. She sparkled and she charmed. Chance thought she was worth every penny and more. She seemed like a diamond stone to him; polished facets reflecting light. Unconquerable. But reaching for her was irresistible.

The night and the clothes wiped out several months' of savings for him. He managed a kiss on the doorstep; she was controlled, skillful, more than merely pleasant. He caught fire, but she pushed him back lightly, spun on her heel, and was gone, door shut.

On Monday, Gus and Judy had more warnings,

"She's no better than her brother. She'll take you for a gold plated ride. You'd be better off using that money to go to school, and going with some nice girl."

Chance said, "I think you're right about school. I wonder if I could work part time, and start taking classes?"

"Sure." said Gus. "You taking something practical?"

"Business and finance." answered Chance.

"There's money in that alright." said Gus.

Judy looked a little sad, "Are you sure that's what you want to do?"

Chance shrugged.

The following weekend Victoria wanted to go into the city to the theatre, then to dinner. Chance bought the tickets and made reservations at the restaurant she requested. She wouldn't go in his old truck, so they took her Mustang. She drove.

Their seats were in the balcony.

"At least we're not behind a pillar." said Victoria, "But why did you get seats way up here?"

Chance didn't tell her it had to do with price. They saw a lavishly successful musical. Chance was carried away to the world the actors were creating. He was suspended from himself. When the lights came up, he struggled to find his footing in his mind.

He was distracted and dreamy the rest of the evening. For once he had no sagging feeling when presented with a richly laden bill. Victoria was delighted with the play. As he looked into her mocking elegant eyes, he thought he saw an enchanted world,

"I wish I could be included in you." he said, as he watched her sip her champagne.

"Ah!" she said, "You would find yourself alone there."

When they rose from the table, she took his arm and eased her sophistication across the floor, silk whispered, eyes followed.


He started classes in the spring. He ate his crackerdust of business courses and failed to believe the magic equations of finance, but excelled in his grade point average. He learned hard and well. He saw little of Victoria; he couldn't afford her just then.

When he had the time, he canoed the spring thaw on the river with Devon and Jack. The brown torrent ripped them over small dams, and towards swift and secret snags. Nimble arms with brute force, paddles dug hard as spades into the relentless water, edged them past danger. Jack whooped and Devon laughed high and manic. Chance exalted silently.

At the end of school, before the start of summer, Chance met Grace and Marina in Washington. He took Victoria with him.

When he saw Grace she seemed frail and wan to him. When he took her in his arms and held her tenderly, he could feel each rib and vertebrae through her flowery dress. She looked up at him, smiling, and wiped a tear from her eye.

"You look thin, tired." she said. 'But you look so good to these old eyes."

He turned to Marina, who hugged him in a bounce. They rocked back and forth. At the moment, she had a body like a dumpling, with impossibly long legs going every which a way. Her hair was chaotic and her glasses slipped down her nose. She perpetually knocked over and into everything. She didn't care; she had hold of life with both hands and was keen with the joy of it. As they hugged, Chance could smell home in his mind- the river, the hydrangeas, the hot wet air.

Chance introduced Victoria, proud that they should see him at the side of such a jewel. They, being women, perhaps saw her differently.

"There's a French restaurant on DuPont Circle that is supposed to be exquisite." said Victoria.

"Darling, we can't be doing that." said Grace gently and firmly.

"Why not?" asked an astounded Victoria.

"We're not that kind of people." she said simply.

The winds blew hot and cold on Chance that week. He divided his time-going to the National Zoo with Marina, Dumbarton Oaks garden with Grace, and an avant garde theatre in the round with Victoria.

After the first night Victoria told him that she required a room at the Hyatt. For once Chance said "no". He did not want to be apart from Grace and Marina.

"Grace is a quaint creature, isn't she?" said Victoria, then continued without waiting for a reply, "And Marina, what a doughty little pumpkin." She paused and added, "I didn't say bumpkin."

"I have knocked your brother down for less than that." said Chance. She slid her eyes sideways and looked up at him from under wickedly lowered lids.

The day Chance took Grace to Dumbarton Oaks; they strolled through the quiet haven of a garden in the midst of the Georgetown bustle.

"Are you happy?" she asked him quietly.

"Happy enough, I reckon. I'm keeping my eye on the prize and working my way in that direction."

"And the prize is?"

He sighed an inward breath, and then sighed a breath outward. "Oh a bright financial future, prestigious career, you know."

"No, I don't know. I don't know this man you want to become. Do you think your goal is worthy?"

Chance paused and then said firmly, "No. But I want it. Or rather I want what it can bring me." He trailed off.

She looked at him sadly. He said, "I thought you would be proud of me!"

"No you didn't." she answered. There was no judgment in her voice, only clarity-and no lack of tenderness.

The day at the zoo with Marina was startling. Every animal responded to her. She seemed to call them by their secret silent names, and they came to her. Chance thought he saw them comforted in their imprisonment, by her presence.

As they conversed about the animals around them, the flowering of her mind became apparent to him. It seemed she had read every word written, if it had to do with those she called "our fellow creatures."

"Well my creature." he said to her, "Let's go get a cold drink. It's getting hot and the smell is really getting rank."

"I like it." she said. "It smells like life!"

They sat on a bench in the shade and talked about home and about Buddy and Grace.

Chance said, "Does Grace seem a little thin to you?"

"She's slowed down." answered Marina. "She's tired-Buddy worries about her, but she says it's just age catching up with her."

"Do you think she'll be lonely when you leave for college?"

"I don't know. I know she misses you like the devil, although she would never say so. Can't you come home for the summer? We all miss you so much."

No, I can't. I'm going to take summer classes. I'm trying to get through as fast as I can."

"Then what? A suit? A city? You've never cared about money. What is this?"

They were sitting next to the giraffe enclosure, and as Chance formulated an answer to Marina, a giraffe waved its head over them, high above on a stem-like neck. It was chewing its cud meditatively, and then with careful thought, spit on Chance's head-a huge slimy warm hat of saliva. As he looked up, spit dripping onto the shoulders of his shirt, the giraffe seemed to give him a small smile. Then the animal bowed down his head and breathed a warmth, sweet hay smelling, into Marina's ear. She stroked the giraffe's cheek. The giraffe faded back up into the heavens.

Chance rubbed his head dry with his tee-shirt and wore the slimy shirt home on the bus. When he entered the room, Victoria looked at his stiffly standing hair and asked, "Did you get a mousse?"

"No, A giraffe." he said.

Chance did not see Marina being awarded third place at the National Science Fair. Victoria was attending a gallery opening on the same evening. He could not afford to lose footing with her, so he chose.

"Are you enjoying having your southern side rubbed by your sweet little family?" she asked.

"You cut too close!" he snapped, but he didn't back away. She gave him that ocelot-in-ice look that always gripped his desire. She turned and pointed to a piece in the show. It was a chrome bumper mounted on the wall. Up close, Chance saw that the artist had managed to create a reflecting-ball effect in the chrome, reflecting objects that weren't there-a orange bridge and a river contorted strangely on the curve of the bumper.

"What a brilliant concept. I love this man's work." said Victoria. She gestured toward the bumper again and said, "This is the future."

A man standing next to them replied, "But my dear, it lacks depth."

"But it's chic!"

"It's a polished work." commented Chance. The man laughed while Victoria shot Chance a quick dagger. The man introduced himself as Jack Evans. Victoria grew respectful. They chatted about the pieces in the show, Evans being far more interested in Victoria's views than Chance's. Chance stood closer to Victoria, Victoria edged a little half step away. Chance suggested it was time to go. She said, somewhat imperiously,

"Oh just a little while longer."

Evans suggested, "Maybe we could go have a drink someplace?"

"No." said Chance, "We need to be getting back."

"You're not going to deny a lovely lady like this an evening out!"

"Some other time." said Chance shortly. Victoria almost didn't go with him. As they ushered out the door and Chance hailed a cab, she hissed,

"Do you have any idea who that was?"

"Yes, an asshole." said Chance.

"That was Jack Evans, senior senator from Connecticut. I can't believe you turned him down!"

"Somebody had to." said Chance dryly.

"That might have been my opportunity." she said.

"He certainly thought it was his." Chance wished he was already in his career. He imagined the threats would be less. They didn't speak during the remainder of the cab ride.

At the hotel, Marina and Grace were shedding rays of happiness.

"You will never believe!" squealed Marina, rushing toward Chance. She hugged him and said, "I got a full four year scholarship to the best marine biology department in Florida!"

Grace beamed and beamed.

"You earned it, Marina." Chance said. "You earned it and I am so proud of you."

She showed them her ribbon and certificates. Victoria glanced at them briefly, congratulated her, and went to bed.

It was their last night together and the three of them sat up late, tying every moment together on a string, holding fast. Early the next morning Chance went with them to the airport, while Victoria slept in. After they said "good-bye" at the gate, Marina turned back to him and said,

"I'm going to tell you what Buddy said when he heard you were going into finance. He said, "There will always be bean counters, stew-nots and shit kickers among us, but that doesn't mean Chance has to be one of them."

She turned and went through the gate.

When they returned to New York State, Victoria withdrew from him once more. He also found, to his irritation, half his classes in the summer semester were electives. He chose cinematography and French. Both courses quickly became far more interesting than the business classes. He had a quick gift for language, the French seemed second nature.

The first day of cinematography class, his teacher, Mr. Bowden, placed six super-eight movie cameras on a table in the front of the room. He broke the group into six pairs and told them to make a three minute movie, right there on the spot. Chance found himself in harness with Shep Sansaveur, a history major who was in his senior year.

Shep said, "If you can whistle, I can juggle."

Chance picked up the camera and began to whistle "Sheep May Safely Graze". Shep grabbed a small spray bottle, a pencil sharpener and a coffee mug off the teacher's desk.

"Roll it!" he yelled. He juggled the spray bottle and pencil sharpener in one hand, sipped coffee from the mug with the other, and did a peculiar slow-jig with his feet to the tune Chance was whistling. When he finished the coffee, he tossed the mug into the air, spun around and continued to juggle. At two minutes and thirty seconds of filming, he dropped the mug, it shattered explosively. Chance kept filming but changed his whistling to "I Sit and

Watch As Tears Go By". Shep danced backwards in retreat from the seriously irate teacher who advanced yelling,

"That was my favorite cup, you moron!"

Shep tossed the spray bottle and pencil sharpener to the teacher, bowed; and Chance stopped filming.

After Mr. Bowden watched the film, he turned to them and said, "I would cheerfully sacrifice ten thousand cups." The little movie was distilled Zen- the essence of pencil sharpener, the wholeness of shattering. Chance had captured it with a zoom and a pan and a quickness ahead of the moment.

"Here we have the proof of what I will try teach you this semester." announced Mr. Bowden to the class. "The camera can capture more than the moment holds. Chance here has done it instinctively. There is a lot of smoke and mirrors involved in movie making but if you are good, you can make people believe that the two dimensions of celluloid are deeper than three dimensional reality. I want each of you to show up here next class with a five minute screen play. See you Thursday."

Chance and Shep walked out together, talking excitedly. Chance felt switched on in places inside of his mind that had never seen light. Shep was full of ideas for screen plays. They walked across campus talking about movies, music, school. Shep was from the Midwest, and lived on campus. They decided to meet the next day after class and work together on creating their screen plays.

On Chance's way home, he stopped at a pawn shop and bought an old super-eight movie camera. He then stopped five times on the way home, to film little scenes that caught his eye- a child bouncing a red and white ball on the cracked sidewalk in front of a house; two sparrows squabbling in a bird bath; water from a leaking hose running into the gutter and showing the reflection of the tree leaves above. He lay awake that night wondering what these new small movies would look like on the screen; if the camera had caught what he thought he saw.

The next day he skipped his European Finance class and went to Mr. Bowden's classroom. Mr. Bowden was grading papers. He showed Chance how to use the projector and the two of them looked at what Chance had filmed the day before. Mr. Bowden asked him if he had ideas about editing. Chance did-and Mr. Bowden knew he had found the kind of clay a teacher dreams of.

Chance and Shep met the next afternoon. Shep lent a spare bicycle to Chance, and they rode up the steep hills together. Coasting down hills, less breathless, they earnestly discussed ideas. Thoughts and sweat poured out in equally copious quantities. By the end of the ride they had hashed out two good storylines.

Chance wrote one of them at work the next morning. Gus and Judy were generous and encouraged him to study whenever business was slow. He wrote a very funny story about a snow shovel and a leaf rake falling in love, and the hilarious cultural misunderstandings-the shovel being winter-souled and the rake autumn.

At the next film class, Shep unveiled a brilliant screenplay using origami figures, describing the life of a Japanese farming family. It was beautiful, erudite and unique. Mr. Bowden again teamed Shep and Chance together, and asked them to film Shep's screenplay.

Chance still made time to run the river with Devon and Jack. They usually ate dinner at Devon's parents afterward. Devon's youngest brother, Danny, hung on every word when the young men told of their adventures on the river.

"I wish I could go with you next time." He said hopefully.

"Squirt, you're too puny for men's work." Devon was dismissive. Danny sat back in his chair, hiding the hurt.

Chance spoke, "Maybe there's something else we can all do."

"Yes, let's go to the quarry." said Victoria. "It's getting hot enough. That would be exciting!"

I don't know if Danny is old enough for that." said his mother.

"Oh mom, sure he is." said Devon, "You can't baby him forever."

"Yeah." chimed in Danny, "I'm big enough, aren't I, Devon?" He looked at his hero, hopeful again.

"Sure you are, Squirt. Anything this old salty cracker can do, I'm sure you can do double." Devon gave Chance that overly hard punch in the arm. As he sat rubbing his arm, Chance looked at Victoria and said,

"I'd like to make a movie of you."

"I'm sure you would." leered Devon.

Chance had learned to ignore Devon, "I'd like to film you as you go about your daily life-a documentary of Victoria."

Victoria found the idea very pleasing. Chance knew she would be compelling on film. He filmed her for the next month; he caught her beauty, wit, elegance, and unknown to her, her cruelty and self-absorption. He felt he was filming the facets of a diamond. The brilliance burnt his eyes, but the edges cut his heart as often.

In the course of filming, he regularly caught interactions with her family; Danny was frequently in the film. When Devon wasn't around, Danny was a funny little spitfire, rascally but harmless. In the presence of Devon, Danny was always desperately treading water reaching for Devon's approval. Devon took it as his due and was stingy with Danny. Victoria remained aloof from the fraternal drama.

Occasionally Victoria would go to Mr. Bowden's classroom, to watch some of the footage of her film. Chance showed her only that which would please her.

One evening Chance took her home and returned to the classroom to continue editing. Mr. Bowden was still there.

"She'll never let you keep filming if she sees what you are holding back."

"I probably won't use most of that." replied Chance, thinking that he meant it.

Shep had come into the room, "I'll bet you twenty dollars you can't resist-it's too good to leave out, it will make the film."

"You're on!" grinned Chance, "Why would I risk losing her? I can barely hold on as it is!"

"Why indeed?" echoed Shep.


Their origami film was progressing into a well-crafted short film. Shep made the folded paper figures and provided all the voices. Chance brought movement to the still figures through his filming techniques. Mr. Bowden had difficulty containing his excitement.

Chance was churning day and night. He had to keep his grades up to keep his financial assistance. He put in as many hours as he could at Gus' store, to pay for food and rent, and to fuel his film habit. He was filming or thinking about filming, continuously.

He ran at full maximum and he loved it. He toyed with the idea of abandoning finance and throwing himself wholly into film making.

All Victoria said to that idea was, "Sayonara. Call me when I'll be returning your call at a Beverly Hills area code."

He decided to continue with investment banking. He found the courses a do-able chore, but he was struggling to ignore the uneasy irritation he felt from the underlying values that oozed through the cracks of his textbooks.

One Saturday morning in August, Devon woke Chance by thwacking him on the leg with a wet towel. "Yo, Salty, rise and shine. Let's go to the quarry, have a little fun."

Chance kneaded the red spot on his calf and said, "I can't. Shep and I are working on the film today."

"Oh, let that pansy fold paper by himself. We can take your truck and get Victoria and Danny on the way." Chance let himself be talked into it.

As Devon walked out of his room he said over his shoulder, "Might want to leave that camera home; gonna be some scrambling involved."

They drove up through the hardwood trees, snaking up a rutted dirt road. After an hour's drive they came to a makeshift parking lot: a handful of miscellaneous jalopies, and beer cans here and there; some of them from a generation before.

The edge of the quarry was steep, and on the way down they slid and grabbed at saplings. A dead tree broke in Devon's hand and sent him sliding into Jack, who cursed and smacked him on the shoulder, then continued to work his way down to a set of ledges. They stood and looked down at the lake twenty feet below. Encased in the steeply rising cliffs, the water was deep, blue, fathomless. A flatness of rock skirted part of the way around the edge of the water. Small groups of young men and women were dotted along the rock with blankets, towels and beer cans.

Devon and Jack greeted a few old acquaintances as they walked to an open spot to spread their towels. Danny stuck proudly to Devon's side.

"Come on, Devon, let's go swimming." He was hopping around, getting in the way. Devon and Victoria were annoyed by him.

"Go ahead, Squirt! Salty will go with you; I'm going to soak up some sun first."

In a burst of boyish enthusiasm, Chance had a water fight with Danny. Then he hoisted him up piggy-back and they had chicken fights with a group of boys. Danny was triumphant whenever he knocked a pair of boys off balance. They straggled back to the edge of the rock and flopped panting and laughing onto their towels.

Victoria said to Danny, "I'm glad you found someone your own age to play with."

Chance laughed, but Danny's joy evaporated and he nudged Devon with his toe.

"Hey Devon, come on, let's you and me go swimming!"

"Squirt, I don't swim in the kiddy pool. The big boys here, we do diving." And he pointed to a ledge twenty feet above the water where three young men were gathered.

"How did they get there?" asked Danny.

"They climbed, stupid." said Devon. "Me and Jack are about to go do the same. Salty, you coming?"

"I am." said Victoria. Chance looked over at her.

"She does it all the time," said Devon dismissively. "She's got bigger balls than most of the boys around here."

"If I were to dignify that with an answer, I'd have to say 'so does a gerbil'." said Victoria.

The climb wasn't as bad as it looked, and there was enough room on the ledge for all five of them. Devon immediately dove in, straight and strong, casual and unstressed. Victoria went next: knifelike, flawless. As he watched, her archetypal female image seared into Chance's brain. Jack jumped feet first and made a resounding splash when he hit. Danny shouted, "Devon, watch me!" his fear hidden only from himself. He leapt holding his nose, then wrapping into a ball and whacking into the water.

He came up sputtering and panicky and too excited, "Did you see that, Devon, did you see that? I did a cannonball!"

"You almost did a bellyflop, but screwed that up." snickered Devon. Jack, treading water next to him, laughed. Victoria was already swimming back to shore and Danny dogpaddled after her.

"Did you see me, Victoria? Did you see me jump?" he pleaded.

"Yes I saw you. You're a brave little boy for your age, but you need to learn how to enter the water."

"I'm not a little boy." he said, exasperated.

"Well, next time jump like a big boy. Keep your body straight and your toes pointed."

Danny had struck the water hard and was too sore to sit down.

Chance still stood on the edge of the ledge. Devon taunted him from the water below, his voice echoing throughout the quarry. Chance could see heads turning his way, as he tried to push his stomach back down out of his throat. He pushed his fear away from him and jumped feet first, before the fear could grab him again. Falling through the air, fear, thrill, wonder at the lightness of the air-he was galvanized. Then his toes touched the water, and the plunge into heavy dark coldness drove everything but panic from his mind. He felt paralyzed as he pressed ever downward-ever darker. It seemed to be forever before he realized he could move his arms and legs, and fight against the gravity sucking him down. He burst through the surface skin of water, his lungs exploding. Still a yell burst forth from him, an uncontrollable celebration of air, sky, and breath. He would have liked to act like Danny, but Victoria hadn't even looked up when he jumped. Devon told him he jumped like a girl.

He pulled himself out of the water and lay down next to Victoria, her skin still cool from the water. He stroked the hollow of her back, and was glad the last five minutes were over.

Devon got up and said, "Let's do some real diving now. Follow me."

Victoria said, "I'll come up, but I'm not diving from there."

"You scared?"

"Yes." she said.

Chance was uneasy as he followed Devon and Jack to the steep-sided rock. They began climbing, finding small handholds, and crumbling spots to place a foot here and there. He could hear Victoria waiting behind him, but he could not climb any faster. Jack was getting further ahead of him, and Chance was having trouble finding places to grab onto. They had climbed about thirty feet before he realized Danny was climbing behind Victoria.

He said, "Danny's coming up!"

Victoria shrugged, concentrating on keeping her weight on her feet. "He's like a little monkey, he'll be alright."

Finally, they all reached an outcropping about forty feet above the water. Devon was hardly winded from the climb, but the rest of them had shaking legs. They were practically at the top of the quarry wall.

Chance asked Victoria, "If you're not going to jump, are you planning to climb back down?"

"No." she laughed. "There's a short trail up to the top from here. Danny and I can climb up, and walk back around to the parking lot."

Devon looked Chance in the eye and said,

"You ready?"

"I don't know. It's mighty high." said Chance, terrified as he looked over the edge. "Have you ever jumped off this?" he asked Devon.

"Once or twice." answered Devon. "It's only for real men. Too much of a wuss?"

"Maybe." replied Chance. He stood at the edge and wrapped his toes on the stone. He stared down, he looked out, he tried to push his fear away but he could not do it.

"No," he said, stepping back. "It's too high. Come on, Champ," he said to Danny, "you can walk back with Victoria and me."

Danny said, "I don't want to be like you, I want to be like him," and he pointed at Devon. Then he walked to the edge and jumped.

Victoria cried out a long anguished wail, "Oh noooo." They watched his small body plummet like a stone, and saw him fall sideways, striking the water hard. They watched the dark shape, surrounded by bubbles as it disappeared down to the depths. Chance waited three gulping breaths of eternity, and then without further hesitation, he leapt off the cliff, and somehow kept his length long and his toes pointed. He sliced into the water thinking only of Danny.

He heard the roaring thumps as Devon, then Jack, entered the water. This time he instantly remembered to move his arms and legs, but this time he was diving downward, searching with his eyes, trying to look through the murky water to see the little boy. He saw darkness, and saw Jack and Devon also frantically searching. His lungs were exploding when he climbed to the surface. He caught huge sucking breaths then dove again, frantic but unbelieving that they would not find him, and haul him up to life and light again.

They did not find him.

His body was found the following day, floating near the rocks where they had basked in the sun.

The entire town turned out at the visitation. When Chance was entering the funeral home, he encountered Devon.

"I don't know why you are coming here." snarled Devon. "It's your fault that he's dead. If you hadn't been such a coward, he never would have jumped."

"Now you know that's not true." said Gus, who was coming up the stairs behind Chance.

"Why don't you shut up and mind your own business, old man!" snapped Devon.

"Chance didn't have anything to do with it. It was just an accident." By now people were gathering around them. Someone tried to pat Devon on the shoulder to calm him, but he shrugged the arm off.

"I want everyone here to know, this is Chance's fault. He killed my little brother." Devon leapt toward Chance and tried to grab him by the neck. Several men caught hold of Devon's arms and pulled him back. He was snarling, rabid, out of his mind,. He twisted and shouted, then suddenly slumped, head dangling, tears pouring down his cheeks.

"He's overcome with grief." said one of the women standing nearby.

Gus clapped his big hand around Chance's elbow, and navigated him into the chapel. "Don't pay any heed to what that poor devil is saying. His conscience must be hurting him something awful."

They entered the stifling flower-heavy room. The little white coffin was open and Chance came near to say goodbye. Danny was dressed in a favorite tee shirt and dungarees, sneakers on his feet, hair sweetly combed. But his face and hands made Chance gasp. Drowning had bleached his face strangely, and changed the texture of his nose and lips. It was almost as if, when he ceased to breathe air and began to breathe water, he started to transmute from boy to fish. As if his spirit had tried, through his body, to feel at home in this new element.

Chance stepped back from the coffin, and Victoria stepped toward it. She bent and kissed her brother's face. The cold living kissed the cold dead.

As Chance watched her, she seemed to be a glass ornament, frosted, glimmering. And suddenly in his heart, that ornament imploded. Silently. Raining a small ashy dust to the ground. He felt empty and numb.

That night Devon threw Chance's possessions out the window of the apartment, onto the street below. Chance heaped them into the back of his truck, and slept on Shep's floor in the dorm room.

He met Victoria in the park the next day. He could not go to her house, Devon was implacable.

"It's over with us." she said.

"I know. Can I do anything to help you?"

"No, just leave us alone. There is no help; we must live now with who we are, and the knowledge that we lost him because we did not care enough to keep him.

"That's not fair." said Chance.

"Life's not fair." said Victoria.

"What will you do?" he asked with pity.

"Go somewhere where no one knows me, where no one pities me." she said. "Probably Boston, some law office. Now Bystander, please go, there's nothing to see here." She smiled her old mocking way, jewel hard, hiding the bitterness and the wound.

Buddy told him to come home, Mark told him to come sailing. He did one and then the other. He headed home first.

Grace met him at the door, took his face in her hands and looked searchingly into his eyes; like a doctor assessing the damage of a wounded man. She said, "My poor dear boy."

Buddy said, 'Welcome back." and gave him a beer.

In the sweet solace of their affection, and the safe familiarity of their company, he pulled the shafts and shards from the wreckage.

"I can't seem to piece any sense out of it." Chance said to Buddy one day as they worked at the garage.

"I don't guess that's going to be easy." Buddy replied. "It might take a long time, and quite a bit more living. Death's a solemn thing-it can't be tasted lightly."

"Do you think Danny's death was my fault?"

"No, I don't." was Buddy's instant response. "But," he said, after a pause, 'you can't keep bad company and not get caught up in bad troubles."

Chance went down to the river that evening. He stood waist deep and then leaned forward and floated with his arms out. He thought about the water; how innocently it held him, how gently. He rolled over and looked at the sky as he floated. And he learned something that has no words; a little peace eased into his mind and he felt his body relax in the embrace of the river.

Later that week he was helping Grace weed the front flower beds. Marina was gone away to college; Grace said her yard help was gone. The asters and Joe Pye Weed were blooming, and butterflies dabbled between blossoms and Grace's big red sun hat. A hummingbird buzzed up and hovered under the brim, looking intently into Grace's eyes, then bolted sideways to visit a Rose-A-Sharon bush.

Grace sat down in the middle of the garden to rest. Chance put down his trowel and said to her, "I'm confused. I thought I was in love with Victoria, but love can't end just like that, in a second, can it?"

"No, but an illusion can." she said.

"I was in love with an illusion?"

"No, you were under the illusion that you were in love."

"I wasn't in love?"

"I don't think so." said Grace quietly. "I think," she leaned forward searching for the words, "when you have a longing for what you imagine a person can give you, you can mistake that longing for love. That's not love, that's desire. It's good to know the difference-desire is about oneself, love is about another."

Chance turned and watched a mourning dove flutter away. The bird's wings made a flustered sound, like a gentle spirit alarmed and fleeing. He turned back to Grace and asked her, "Can't love and desire be there at the same time?"

"Yes," she said, "But sometimes it's just desire calling itself love."

"And what would you call what I was doing?"

"Trying to measure up. You tried to climb her disregard like it was a mountain. You know when a man stands on top of a peak; he's exactly the same height as when he was down below."

Chance laughed ruefully and said, 'You might be right. But, I find this confusing.

"I imagine you do. Desire is like a mirror we hang on someone else. It's hard to reach through the reflection, to go beneath that surface, but that's where love lies."

Chance listened carefully and put her words away where he could find them some future day. That was the best that she had hoped for, when she spoke to him.

She said, "I've done all the work I can for now, I'm going to go lie down for a spell." Her sweet smile was tired, and precious to him.

He stayed with them through September. Then, much patched together, he came into the glory of the New England fall and sailed with Mark on the low Long Island Sound, the Spinthrift leaping like a dolphin over the steep sided peaks and valleys of the sea.

He spent his evenings with Mark and Marie. Marie unbent towards him, moved by the tearing of the tragedy. She was genuinely interested in his budding world of film-making. She drew him out, distancing him from the darkness he was holding.

They took him to an Independent Film House in a town nearby. From then on, he wallowed in a feast of foreign films, going almost every night.

The sea washed and cleaned the wounded past, healing what could be healed. The wind cut to the bone, blowing away the false mists of the confusion that could be found.

Other dark shapes sunk out of sight inside of him.

At the same time, his mind- a riotous expanding jumble fed on the mastered pieces of decades of film. New coves and meadows opened continually in his mind; leaving no time to stand in his own past.

And yet, some nights he awoke from sleeping-or did he dream that he awoke? Danny stood in his doorway, dripping and pale. He never spoke or beckoned-just looked at Chance with fathoms of a forlorn unasked question. Chance spoke to the vision, asked him what he wanted but Danny never spoke or changed his expression. The mornings after these visitations, Chance would check the floor in the doorway as if the absence of moisture would prove something.

One day as they sailed along on a wide reach, breezes barely blowing for a change, Mark spoke,
"Marie has suggested that I make a loan to you."
"That's mighty nice of her, but what do I need a loan for?"
"To make a film." said Mark.
Chance sat on the rail and stared at Mark who stood steering the boat, his hand on the wheel. Spindrift's wake was paving a path of sunlight on the sea behind him. The bluest sky above framed Mark's face and torso. Chance felt like the golden sunlight on the water was a path opening at his feet.
He said, "I feel like I could walk on the water right now."

Chance called Shep in upstate New York; Shep immediately became a partner in the upcoming film. Shep said, "Devon and Jack have gone off to the oil fields of Oklahoma and Victoria has gone to Boston, so there is peace in the valley tonight."

"Hallelujah to that." said Chance. "Speaking of Victoria, I want to make a film out of all that footage I shot last year."

"It's great footage, you can make a hell of a film out of it, but......"

Chance interrupted, "I wonder if you would be willing to cut all the footage of Danny, and put it in a separate can. I don't really want to see it right now."

"Sure man, no problem." Shep had every minute of his time full past overflowing, he was planning to graduate in six weeks with a double major in American history and film-making; but somehow, Danny's image had disappeared from the footage when Chance arrived a week later.

Chance began the final editing of the Japanese origami short-film that had been abandoned after Danny drowned. Mr. Bowden worked with him, teaching him how to trim raw footage into a tight little film. Chance worked fast, putting in long hours every day. Shep had to turn the film in for his final grade. Mr. Bowden was chuckling as he put the small can holding the final cut into Shep's folder.

"This little baby is a jewel."

Chance went straight into working on the "Victoria" film. When he was finished it was black and white, forty five minutes long, and sterling.

Mr. Bowden was silent after seeing it for the first time. He turned to Chance and said,

"It's unbelievably good, but are you sure you want to show it?"

Chance said, "Yes, it's my work."

Mr. Bowden said, "It ought to be shown, it's a superb film, but are you sure you want to expose this woman in this way? She's obviously heartless, she shows us that in the film, but still-it lays her soul, or soullessness, bare. Are you sure you want to do this?"

"Yes." said Chance.

Shep shook his head. "Don't you want to put it in the can and when you're famous, it can come out as the discovered early work of a genius?"

"I don't know what you-all are making such a fuss about. She'll never see it. It will get shown at a couple of little juried shows and then be retired to the back of my closet."

While Shep finished up school, Chance built a plywood shell for the back of his pickup; and with Mr. Bowden's help, located good used equipment from filmmaker's magazines. He bought a covered trailer, and the day after Shep graduated they headed south through the snow, the trailer skidding and bumping with all their precious gear. They were relieved to get out of the Snow Belt. They had dry roads and high times all the way to Florida. They had no script written, but they had decided a warm winter location would be a great place to make their first real movie.

They developed the plot as they drove, Shep scribbling as fast as he could to catch their ideas.

"So, we'll have a half-crazy beach-combing girl who is learning meditation from an old, culturally clueless Buddhist monk in an orange robe. The two of them will jail break the girl's grandmother from a nursing home and take her on a prolonged road trip in a travel trailer. The old lady hasn't lived in the modern world for fifty years, and the monk is basically an old remittance man from South East Asia, who was legitimately mindful some time ago, deep in the jungle. He also has a hell of a healing chant act worked up."

Let's have a dog in it, too." said Chance.

"Yeah, an orange Chinese Chow dog to go with the monk." added Shep.

Once they crossed the state line into Florida, they turned off of the highway and rambled back roads, working their way south. Shep sang the Boll Weevil song,

"Just a lookin' for a home, just a lookin' for a home," and made up verses as they drove through miles of orange orchards and occasional flat pasture filled with boney looking cows and a sparse palmetto tree. They came to the edge of a little town named Orange Blossom, and Shep whistled. "This may be the place!"

Little houses tin roofed, wooden sided, sweet and simple from a generation before. They stopped at the filling station-general store that was complete with three old timers rocking on the front porch. They were invited to pull up a chair. In the next hour they heard about the river, fish, the gators, the beach, fish, the canal, fish. Next they were invited home to meet the family of one of the codgers. Shep said, "I think this IS the place!"

"Atmospheric perfection." sighed Shep happily.

Orange Blossom rested calmly in damp primordial time, roofs shingled in silvery tin glinting dully back at an opaque sky. Shep and Chance arrived in the winter when crisp air brought estivating citizens to movement and large migratory birds came back to roost. Someone in town quickly rented them a travel trailer and someone else gave them a spot on a backwater, hung with Spanish moss. Lotus-like lilies flowered in the still water and wildlife abounded, including a few resident alligators who were unobtrusive unless tempted by the presence of cats or small dogs. Shep and Chance moved right in, planning to vacate during filming, when the trailer would act as the primary set in their movie. Shep got down to actually writing some of the dialogue while Chance explored locations.

Marina was attending a college that was about two hours' drive from Orange Blossom. She came to visit a few weeks after they settled in. As she got out of her car in front of the trailer, Shep said incredulously, "That's Marina?"

"I think so." said Chance, stunned. "I saw her six months ago and she didn't look like THAT!"

Marina had moulted and fledged almost overnight. Her movement seemed to carve a slight glow in the air. The two men each wished they had combed their hair, as they watched her walking toward them over emerald lush grass. Then, eyes and mouth, she smiled; and neither man thought of anything but her. Chance hugged her saying, "Oh my beauty! Where has the little girl gone?" He held her away from him, and then hugged her to his chest again. He introduced her to Shep, who took her hand and returned her sweet smile.

"Want to be in pictures?" he immediately asked.

She laughed and said, "No thanks, but you're a darling to ask."

"You'd make our fortune for us." he said.

She just smiled and shook her head. He shook himself, and then said "Welcome to Spanish Moss Productions!"

Chance wrapped his arm around her shoulders, Shep grabbed her bag, and they showed her into the travel trailer. They talked for hours, all three of them talking at once, sometimes. Marina joined right into the plans, dreams and plot of the movie they were beginning. Then they talked about her work at school, she was doubling up with animal behavior and marine biology.

"I've started helping with a study of a protected oxbow on the river, near school. It's a new approach to animal behavior. We're watching all the different species in a small designated study area, trying to see the system as a living whole, instead of focusing on one kind animal, isolating its behavior and seeing it as separate from the natural world it lives in and the other animals around it.. It's really fascinating. I watched a possum and a black snake have an all-out wrestling match last weekend. The snake kept trying to get away and the possum kept coming after it. The snake finally did get away into a dead tree trunk and out the other side. I didn't know if the possum was hunting the snake, or just didn't like his looks!"

Shep laughed and said, "Maybe we can cast them in the movie."

Chance spoke less than usual that evening. He listened to Marina and Shep; and watched as Marina moved her hands as she spoke and leaned forward to share a joke with Shep. Her transformation stunned him. She, as a woman, was who he loved. She glanced over at him with the same look in her eyes that she had always had for him; in a flash he knew she had been waiting a long time to become the woman he loved. Shep, being a true friend, had seen immediately what it had taken Chance years to learn.

The next day Marina went back to the coast and her "swamp" studies as Shep called them. She was commissioned by them to acquire a red chow dog with as biddable a nature as possible. The two men got down to the business of making a film.

Shep set up a card table on the porch of the general store among the cracker-barrelers, and the auditions began. It seemed that everyone in town wanted to be an actor. The script was left intentionally loose to allow room for any unexpected talents or great hilarity that might show up on the porch. The regular rocking curmudgeons remained on the porch and served a useful function, their presence deterred anyone with stage fright or even nervous sensitivities. They did their job well, heckling and editorializing in a not too unkind fashion.

The first unexpected pleasure was James Mullican, a middle-aged black man of some girth and dignity. Shep engaged him in conversation while Chance studied his face and natural movement, and listened to his voice.

Shep said, "The part we want you for is, unfortunately, a small one."

"I don't mind." said James. "I'm just curious about the whole process and would like it very much if I could play a part in it." His voice was deep and sonorous; his face was calm and reflective.

Shep, looking up at him said, "The role is a doctor in a free clinic, dealing with a culturally illiterate Buddhist monk who has some attitude problem with race."

"Is this monk Asian?" asked James.

"Yes he is."

"And he has attitude about race?"

"Yep."

"That shouldn't be a problem. I've encountered 'attitude' before, I don't believe it was ever in an Asian wrapper, tho."

During the rest of the afternoon, they cast many people for minor roles: nursing home staff and various characters along the way. As Shep was folding up his card table at the end of the day, Dan, the keeper of the general store said, "I don't know if they would do it, but from what you two fellows have been saying about this story you-all are going to film, you might oughta go see Sylvia and Miss Margaret."

"Really?" asked Chance.

"Yeah, really! If they would agree, I imagine they would be just about perfect."

"Where would we find these two perfections?" asked Shep.

Dan pointed up the road that teed into the highway in front of his store. "Quarter mile or so up there. Only house there, you can't miss it."

They thanked him for the tip and went up the road on their bicycles. They did soon come to the end of the road and there was only one house there.

"Holy Moly! Shades of Faulkner!" said Shep. They were facing an exhausted, much columned and porched, hip-settled beauty. Unvisited by Sherman, bedecked in wisteria, white blossoms and blue, a smallish wooden mansion. As they climbed the steps to the porch, Shep commented, "It's not really rotten, not even as frail as it looks."

"Neither am I." said an old woman sitting in a very high-backed rattan chair.

"Well I'm very glad of that, Madam, because we have come to offer you employment," answered Shep quickly, positing this was Miss Margaret, because she certainly looked perfect for the part.

"I would be delighted." she said.

"Aren't you even going to ask what it is?"

"No. I know two intelligent looking young men like yourselves would not squander your time or mine on frivolousness or mischief." Her eyes sparkled and she added, "Unless either was great fun." Miss Margaret was dressed in buttoned-up black yesterday, including lace at her neck and wrists.

"Do your boots button?" asked Shep. Chance poked him in the side.

"Don't be fresh." said Margaret. She rang a small pewter handbell, and a minute later a young woman dressed in white cotton stepped out onto the porch.

"Darling, these two gentlemen are going to take me into their employ."

"In what capacity, Auntie Meg?" asked the young woman, barefoot and honey tumbled.

"Film star." said Shep. "You too."

"This is Sylvia," said Miss Margaret, "my great niece. I didn't catch your names."

"You must be the film makers!" said Sylvia.

Introductions were made, tea was sipped, and a deal was struck. Margaret and Sylvia would be in the movie and in return Chance and Shep would make many repairs on the beautiful ghost of a house.

Under Miss Margaret's patronage Spanish Moss Productions was granted permission to film inside Shady Nook Senior Home. Some of the residents and staff agreed to participate in the film. The greatest problem would be to get the residents to be less cheerful on film, and the staff to evince an inattentive and callous attitude toward the old folk.

"All we need now is our monk." said Shep at the end of the week."

"I might have one for you on Sunday." Chance told him. "Marina found a temple on the coast that serves the Cambodian immigrant population. We're going to meet there and we'll see what turns up."

"Fantastic! While you're doing that, I think I'll go over to Miss Margaret's and swing a hammer for little while."

"Will Sylvia help you?"

"I don't know, but whether she does or not, she'll make the work easier." grinned Shep.

Marina and Chance found the Cambodians and their temple on the run-down edge of the nearby coastal city, where Marina went to school. The men made their living fishing and the women helped in the evening with the catch, when the boats came in. They were all recent arrivals, in the last year or two. Very little English was spoken. The temple was in one side of an old duplex, which had recently been shown loving care from willing hands and empty purses. The living room held the shrine. It was full of shockingly opulent-looking brass Buddhas, happily full of big bellied emptiness.

A middle aged monk approached them, his head shaved and his body wrapped in a burnt- sienna colored robe. He was not built quite so opulently as the Buddha statues he tended. Incense from a comforting spice had softly permeated every nook in the room and perhaps the monk as well. He was welcoming, looking at them through serene eyes.

"I'm Ten Ha." he said. He shook hands with Chance-a soft limp handclasp Chance noted with surprise. Ten Ha bowed to Marina with folded hands and said, "Forgive me; I cannot shake your hand. Monks are forbidden to touch women. Sorry sorry! We don't have many American visitors-may I ask you to meet the monks? They will like it very much. Would you like a cup of tea?"

There was whispering and manly giggling from behind the door into the next room.

"Excuse me." said Ten Ha to his guests, then he slid behind the door and there was a little calm whispering. He re-appeared, followed by a very thin monk marked by great old age and unsteady step. Behind him came a robust monk who looked to be in his early thirties, and finally, someone who was practically a boy, but big and awkward. The very young monk tried to keep his eyes on the ground as he approached, but he kept rolling his eyes up at the visitors and then dropping his gaze back to the floor. The other monks approached with sedate and measured steps, not looking at Chance and Marina until they were facing them. Then the monks, all in a line, bowed to them hands clasped at their hearts. Chance and Marina bowed back, hoping it was the friendly thing to do. Ten Ha looked at the very young monk and nodded. The young man stuffed his hand in his mouth, giggled, and then did a scooting shuffle back into the kitchen. Ten Ha indicated mats and cushions on the floor, and asked them to sit. The monks sat on grass mats and casually tucked their feet into lotus positions under their robes.

Marina curved her legs under her, feet facing behind her. Ten Ha smiled at her and asked,

"Do you know our ways?"

"A little bit." she said. "I've read a few books.

"About Buddha?"

"And about South East Asian cultures."

"Ah. Thank you."

"We have come here for a reason." said Chance.

"Yes, yes. First we will have some tea." said the monk.

The young monk came out of the kitchen carrying a tray heavily laden with teapot, cups, milk, sugar and cookies. He set the tray down in front of the guests. Ten Ha poured the tea and passed cups all around, except Marina's which he set on the floor in front of her. He talked about the temple and the people of his community, whom he had come to serve. He made complimentary, possibly insincere, remarks about American life.

Marina and Chance declined more tea and Ten Ha nodded to the young monk to remove the tray. The other monks rose, smiling and bowing, and left the room.

Ten Ha waited for Chance to speak. Chance told him about the movie, was frank about the less-than–perfect character of the monk in the film, and was equally open about his own depth of ignorance about Buddhist culture. The monk listened, nodded from time to time, and then asked how long this actor would be required.

"Maybe two months at the most. Of course he will be paid and given a place to live in Orange Blossom while we are filming."

Ten Ha closed his heavily lidded eyes and thought for a ticking minute. At last he opened his eyes slowly, and looked at Chance, silent a little longer.

"Do you think I would be good for this?" he asked.

"You?" asked Chance, astonished.

The monk nodded.

"Where could I find better! But can you leave the temple? Who will be in charge? And, I don't know if I can pay the type of salary you might be receiving now."

Ten Ha laughed musically and sincerely. "You have no problem there, my friend. Monks cannot handle money. You do not need to pay me."

"But you will need to feed him," said Marina, "and he will be very sad if you don't feed him what he is accustomed to!"

"No no no, not a problem." protested Ten Ha.

Marina gave Chance a significant look. "He can't prepare his own food. He's not allowed."

"There's a little Chinese restaurant in Orange Blossom. Will that do?"

The monk and Marina looked relieved.

"No problem." said Ten Ha.

"What about the temple?" asked Chance.

"Lu Kah, brother monk can take care of things here. He will be happy. He is Sri Lankan. It will be his first time to be boss. He will like it."

"When can you start?"

"When you will bring me to that place."

"In a few days?"

Ten Ha answered, "In a few days, now, whenever you like."

Marina said, 'I can bring him over next weekend."

As they left, all the monks were bowing to them and smiling.

That evening Marina and Chance walked on the beach as the sun set. It was calm and cool, the beach was deserted. He turned to her and put his arms around her. He looked down at her face then slowly bent his lips to hers and kissed her forever.

"I've been slow." he said.

Marina snuggled her head against his shoulder and said, "No hurry now."

"I want you." he said.

"You'll have me."

"Now?"

"Too many people."

Chance looked around at the empty beach, but said, "I didn't mean right now."

"We could. In the ocean. It's just about dark."

They left their clothes on the sand and waded in until the water was almost shoulder deep. The air was cool but the water was warm. In the sea, her thighs riding his hips, his arms and the ocean's lapping wavelets carrying her, they found their ecstasy in each other. Ancient aquatic physical love, as old and as fresh as each new dawn. As they lay in the gritty sand afterward, velvety and star-ridden, Chance felt a tear under his thumb as he traced Marina's face in the dark.

"What's this?" he murmured as he rolled toward her to kiss the tear away.

"I'm just wondering if there will ever again be a day in my life as perfect as this."

One week later, Marina came to Orange Blossom with a carful of monks and the promised fluffy orange chow dog.

Chance said, "What's all this?" as Ten Ha and dog climbed out of the front seat, and the other three monks poured out of the backseat.

"Monk infestation." said Shep.

"Holiday." said Lu Kah, the Sri Lankan.

Marina said, "They wanted to come see what we were doing. They don't get out much; none of them drive. I think they're not allowed to."

"Shopping." said the young monk floppishly, as he tripped over his large sandaled feet.

"Yes, shopping." said Marina testily, "on the way home." She turned to Chance and said, "A woman at the temple gave me twenty dollars for the monks to buy sundries."

"Reading glasses." explained Ten Ha.

"Music player!" said Boon-ho, the young monk.

The very old monk lit another cigarette and grinned a little toothlessly, crinkling his rheumy eyes. Although his ribs showed and his legs were bandied, his arms still showed ropey hints of a life filled with a great deal of labor.

"Hard working monk." said Chance to Ten Ha, nodding his head to the side at the old man.

"Yes." said Ten Ha. "He just became monk this year. It is customary in our country. He has done his work and raised his family. Now he can withdraw from the world and be monk. His wife lives at the temple, as well. She cooks for us and takes care of her husband."

"A monk can have a wife?"

"No, not really wife anymore. Now she is helping the monk, not the husband."

Chance offered the old man a beer, but Shep shook his head and took the can. "They don't drink."

"Clouds the mind." offered Ten Ha.

The old man went and sat under a live oak tree near the trailer.

"He needs rest." said Ten Ha patiently.

Shep volunteered, "I'll stay here with him and the dog. The rest of you go on in and see the town."

They walked the quarter mile to town. On the way Chance dropped back with Marina and asked, "Are you going back tonight?"

"Yes, this burden of monks has to be back tonight for some special prayers and chanting. They were in the car before I knew it, and they didn't seem to understand me when I tried to get them back out. Anyway, I'm working in the swamp tomorrow, and have to finish a paper by Monday."

Will you be here next weekend?"

"I don't know. I really want to be in the field right now. The study is getting really fascinating."

"Will you marry me?"

"Yes."

They caught up with the monks, who caused a sensation at the general store. Boon-ho yelped, "Shopping!" while for once the habituants of the porch were silent. Ten Ha stood looking at the men sitting in rocking chairs. His hands were folded over his not overly large stomach and he smiled benevolently at the men. Marina thought he looked like a large reddish-brown flower.

"I am Ten Ha, monk of Buddha."

"Are you a fairy?" asked one man curiously.

"I don't know." said Ten Ha with interest.

"Well, you're wearing a dress! And if you-all shaved your heads on account of lice or ring worm, please step off the porch!" said a really grumpy man.

"No lice. Monk haircut." answered Ten Ha happily, as he rubbed his shaved head.

Dan, the store keeper said, "Your barber took a little off the top, didn't he? So where you from?"

"I am from Cambodia, he is from Cambodia, he is from Sri Lanka."

"I guess that's south of Texas, huh?" said one of the men. Then he nodded to an empty rocker and said, "Have a seat."

Ten Ha sat tentatively in a rocker and gently pushed back and let the chair rock forward. The men watched him as he tilted smoothly forward and back. He stopped, got up, and sat on the floor of the porch, crossing his legs in a lotus position, as usual, under his robes.

"He's a regular Houdini." said the grumpy man. In the meantime, Boon-ho got into the chair and commenced rocking furiously, the chair slapping and jumping.

"Whoa there fella, take it easy! You're gonna hurt the chair, and yourself as well." Boon-ho just widened his eyes and mouth, and practically waggled his ears. Ten Ha said something gently. Boon-ho immediately stopped and came to sit quietly next to Ten Ha.

"Sorry sorry!" said Ten Ha. "Boon-ho's mind not fully formed-no room for mindfulness."

"Is he saying that Bruno there is a few bricks short?"

Boon-ho smiled and said, "Not all dots on dice," and tapped his head.

"How on earth did he get all the way over here from where ever it is he comes from?"

"His mother sent him-not enough food at home. He cannot work, so he becomes monk and we take care of him. He helps at temple. He sweeps and cleans, washes monk's clothes and dishes."

Dan said to Marina, "Do you want to bring Bruno inside, let him do a little shopping?" Marina, Boon-ho and Lu Kah went in, and the two monks looked at every single item in the store. Dan said, "I should get them to do inventory for me."

Finally, they put a small pile of merchandise on the counter: some reading glasses, a pen, a pack of cards, and some candy. Marina began to pay for it, but Dan waved her money away. "Nah, this one is on me."

The two monks bowed several times, saying, "Thank you, thank you."

Marina added, "You've just gained merit."

"Gained what?"

"Brownie points in the karma bank, according to their beliefs."

"I have no idea what you're talking about, but get them both a bottle of pop, and put it on my karma account."

"Time to go, boys." said Marina. The monks reluctantly followed her down the stairs.

"You come back any time you want." shouted somebody. The three monks turned around and bowed. As they walked back to the trailer, Ten Ha said,

"Good men. Very kind, very generous to strangers."

Ten Ha and the new dog were staying for now with Chance and Shep in the travel trailer. Marina left, her monks trailing after her.

The chow dog, a female named Tara, had never been off of a leash. She wasn't vicious, but she did bite if someone tried to touch her.

"Great! Is she supposed to sleep with her leash on?" said Chance. Ten Ha clapped his hands softly and bent slightly at the waist, looking at Tara. The dog trotted straight to him, purple tongue relaxed. He reached down gently to her collar and unhooked the leash. Tara sat on his feet.

Shep said, "You'll be working two jobs, you just got elected as dog wrangler."

"No problem." Ten Ha assured him. He snapped the leash back on the dog and started out the door with her.

"First, dog and I will discuss responsibility. After, dog will be ready for freedom." He walked along the lake with her for about an hour. Shep and Chance, watching them in the distance, could see that the monk would talk to the dog from time to time, then reach down and scratch her ears. She looked up at him quizzically when he spoke.

Chance said to Shep, "Monk and dog are going to look very good on the screen. Tara is almost the same color as his robe."

Shep said, ' I think, in terms of Marina, you are very lucky he is a monk. He's like St. Francis reincarnated."

In the distance they saw Ten Ha remove the leash from the dog and suddenly Tara was an orange blur of motion, streaking across the parkland toward them. When she was almost upon them, she spun sharply on her stiff little pins and hurtled herself back to the monk. Back and forth, never slowing, she raced for almost five minutes, until, in a blindness of ecstasy and a lifetime of not running, she crashed straight into the trunk of a young magnolia tree. She rebounded onto her back haunches, eyes glazed, jaws grinning. As she shook her head, Chance said,

"You can practically see the stars circling around her doggy cranium!" As they went to see if she was injured, she hopped up, trotting toward them, unconcerned. "What a rock hard noggin our Tara has."

Her purple tongue hung like a neat pennant from her open jaw, and her shiny black shoe-button eyes were bright again. She plopped down in the grass, on Chance's feet, and looked up at him, breathing hard and happy.

"You'll do." he said.

That night they decided to name the film 'Going Om' and the next day they commenced filming. Chance would have kept the crew and cast working around the clock. He was in a fire of enthusiasm and creativity. But Sylvia would not allow Miss Margaret to be on the set more than six hours a day, including a nap in the middle. Miss Margaret was as excited as Chance and Shep, and would have overtired herself if Sylvia had not been watchful.

Chance's inexperience as a director quickly surfaced. He knew what he wanted to see and hear, but he didn't know how to draw it out of the actors. One day Sylvia blew up at him.

Why don't you just get a bunch of mannequins or ventriloquist dummies? You don't want any of us to express our interpretations, even though we ARE the characters. You treat us like a chess set put here for you to move around."

"I'm trying to create my vision here!" snapped Chance. "And I don't need my concentration broken by an amateur backseat driver. You're here to play the part as Shep wrote it!"

Shep stepped into the argument, 'Chance, this is our vision, not yours alone. Personally I welcome the depth that everyone here is trying to add to their roles. In an effort to get the visual effect you have in your mind, you've been squashing the subtle and intricate dance being created between Barbara, Miss Margaret's character, and the monk.

I think the exquisite complexity- subtle, skillful, of two experienced souls is worth more here than a hundred beautiful shots."

"How can you say that? This is a MOVIE for God's sake; it's all about the visual."

"No. It's also about the feeling, about the relationships of these characters with each other and themselves. The visuals need to be a vehicle to carry these people."

"I don't see it." said Chance.

"Well I do." answered Shep quietly and firmly. Several of the actors nodded their heads in agreement.

Chance looked at Ten Ha who stood silently listening.

"What do you think?" Chance asked him.

"Generosity may be helpful. A leader is necessary, but one person's vision maybe more narrow than collective vision."

Chance and Shep laughed. "Oh you shame me." said Chance lightly.

"No need for shame, just need for sharing. Good lesson."

When they returned to shooting, Chance tried to relax and allow more latitude for the cast. But he continued to concentrate on creating the visual via the camera; and also on getting the actors to deliver their lines in the style that he conceived for each character.

At the end of the day, he, Shep, and Ten Ha sat in lawn chairs outside, in front of the trailer.

"I'm sorry I crowded you today." he said to Shep. "I get so wrapped up in the way I want this movie to be. How I visualize it!"

Shep answered, 'I understand. I feel the same way. But I take a different approach. The script is just a handful of seeds. Our job is to nurture and water-let the characters take shape in the hands of the actors. Granted, we need to prune and weed, to keep chaos at bay, but I think half the quality of this film is going to come out of spontaneous creativity from the actors, and the way they relate to each other in their characters. I think the other half of the quality of this movie is going to be in your brilliant gift for visualizing, then realizing it with the lens.

Chance leaned back and blew his breath out with a frustrated sigh.

"I know you must be right, and I'm looking; but I don't see what you're seeing-these characters involvement with each other outside of the script." He looked over at Ten Ha and raised an eyebrow.

"When not have discernment, might be good idea to use eyes of wise friend."

"Well. I'm going to follow Shep's lead, but you're right, I'm driving in the dark with no headlights on this one. I just hope you two have both eyes burning bright, or we'll end up like those three witches in Lapland, passing one eyeball around in the dark, between the three of them."

Conversation got side tracked immediately, because Ten Ha had never heard of the story or Lapland, and insisted that Chance and Shep tell the myth from a land of snow.

Afterward, Ten Ha sat in the grass, Tara by his side, and began to chant the long sutra of loving-kindness, praising the precious jewel in the lotus, and calling down peace and enlightenment on everybody and everything.

"Whether we want it or not." joked Shep as he listened to the cavernous drone that poured forth from Ten Ha. The sun set slowly and an alligator across the water began booming back in answer to the monk's resonant prayer.

The filming went well through the winter. Miss Margaret and Ten Ha immersed themselves in their roles. Sylvia sparkled on film; she created a character of Zen zaniness that was endearing, funny and intelligent. Chance delighted in filming her, because from every angle she was expressive in new ways. The battles between them were infrequent- Chance bowed to Shep's opinion about the actors' scope when it became an issue.

Shep moved into Miss Margaret's house and Chance soon followed. Ten Ha asked to continue living in the trailer, to enjoy the solitude, and Tara stayed with him. Mr. Bowden came down to be an advisor during his mid-winter break. He brought some startling news.

"I might as well tell you, I entered that little origami film in a festival for short films in Tokyo."

"Okay." said Chance.

"It's been an extraordinary success."

"That's just great." said Shep.

"No. I mean it's created a sensation." persisted Mr. Bowden.

"That's kind of over the top for a simple school project, don't you think? But maybe it will give us a leg up when we're trying to get this film into the Sundance festival."

"Maybe it will pay for this film and your next." said Mr. Bowden.

Shep and Chance were dumbfounded. "How could that possibly be?" asked Chance.

"Japanese children have gone crazy for the characters-the family of farmers. A nationwide noodle shop wants to buy the film and all the merchandizing rights. I took it upon myself to run their proposals by a lawyer who is in this line of work. I have the paperwork with me if you're interested."

"Some McNoodle business wants to merchandise little origami figures designed by Americans?" asked Shep, who then burst out laughing. "What a funny world we live in!"


     The cast took the next day off and Sylvia threw a party to celebrate the new found wealth. Chance went right out and bought an instant rice cooker for Ten Ha. He presented it to him at the party. Shep tried to drink champagne out of Sylvia's tennis shoe, but the champagne ran out the grommet holes, and Tara licked it off the dining room floor. A guitar, a stand-up bass and a fiddle manifested. Which led to a lively jitter-bug being danced through the living room and parlor, unlikely partners smiling and twirling. Ten Ha sat cross-legged on the porch and smiled at everyone as they caroused.
     Miss Margaret came and sat on the glider, next to where he was sitting.
     "Ten Ha, you are such a mindful and well behaved monk; how are you able to play your part in the movie. I don't believe you were ever jaded or greedy or dishonest, like Bundhi is in the movie?"
     "I know this monk very well. I have met him many times. But movie is good because it shows monk can learn and change, become better person. But sometimes knowledge has to sneak up on monk. I like this story very much. Monk help old lady, old lady help monk become more wise. You play lady who is half blind. You not half blind, but you understand this half blind person. Same thing for me. I understand this monk who has mind's eye half blind."
     Miss Margaret smiled and rocked gently.
     "I would have to be more than half blind not to see how well suited Sylvia and Shep are for each other. It's a great pleasure in my old age to see Sylvia happily situated in love.
     "They know each other before." said Ten Ha.

"No, they just met when Shep came here to make "Going Om."

Ten Ha responded, "They are old souls. Know each other a long time, thousand years maybe. Now, they find each other again, and are ready to be happy together."

Miss Margaret wiped the corner of her eyes with a soft embroidered hanky. "That's the sweetest thing to say."

In the morning, most of the crew came back and cleaned up from the party, then got back to work. Mr. Bowden looked at the footage and helped them cut away the extraneous. The two directors were each attached to many scenes that had to go.

"The film is going to be six hours long if you don't get ruthless with yourselves. A lot of these scenes with encounters with minor characters are delightful, funny, wonderful-it's an embarrassment of riches. But, they are diluting this amazing relationship that grows between the three main characters. The damn dog is distraction enough- it looks like a cross between an extra-terrestrial and a stuffed animal."

"I'm glad you feel that way about the dynamics of the main characters." said Shep quietly. "The actors have been digging really deep to get us there!"

"Yeah," added Chance, "and I had to learn to sit on my hands to get us there!"

Winter rolled into spring, the migratory birds flew away and filming came to an end. Chance and Shep stayed on at Miss Margaret's. The house was mostly empty and they had gradually assimilated themselves into the back section of the old manse, until it morphed into their offices and production studio. Ten Ha went back to his temple, contented. He was happy to have a better understanding of the culture around him in his adopted land; and glad to have a connection with some of the natives of this new land. He and Marina had become very good friends. She visited him at the temple when she had a spare hour. Sometimes she brought him to gatherings at the University, where he met people from many of the departments. Chance joked that Ten Ha saw more of Marina than he did. Her workload was heavy and her dedication to her field studies was intense. In addition, she took every available opportunity to get out on the water. And in it as well, snorkeling whenever she had time between samplings and assays.

Chance and Shep, with some help from Sylvia, improved Miss Margaret's house bit by bit, making the project into a hobby. No one was in a hurry.

Income was rolling in from the Japanese Noodle chain, bringing in its wake, the first air conditioners to be installed in Orange Blossom. The back wing of offices, and several bedrooms got units. Miss Margaret wanted nothing to do with it.

"Hot cold hot cold- a person would have the Old Folks' Friend here in no time."

"Old Folks' Friend?" asked Chance.

"Pneumonia! Helps us down the stairs when it's time to go. That air conditioning is going to thin a lot of the crowd at Shady Grove Home, if they put it in there. Don't let any of the Peterson heirs get wind of this contraption. They'll put two or three in their mother's room."

Shep said, "There may be some truth in your theory, but I'm a transplant here-tender and leafy. I think I might get root rot if I don't make myself a cool dry niche in my room."

As the wet summer heat came on, the town lapsed back into slow rocking, shade fishing calm. The excitement of the movie filming became fodder for rumination for the group of locals on the front porch of the general store. Some of the old timers chewed film cud in one cheek and tobacco in the other.

Chance and Shep worked in the studio through the sticky Florida summer. Sometimes, for relief, they dropped the big aluminum canoe into the turgid river, just before dawn, then paddled upstream for an hour as fast and as hard as they possibly could, sweating and panting, exhilarated in the joy of their healthy bodies making a massive effort. Frightened gators beat their tails on the water and sunk below the surface, while white herons flapped screeching from sleep into the dawning air.

When they could paddle no further at their furious rate, they dropped their paddles and slumped over the stanchions, letting the canoe begin a slow drift back down the brown shiny river, half lost in a mist that was beginning to glow with the rising sun light.

As soon as the paddling stopped, the mosquitoes arrived in a whining drone like a miniscule squadron of tiny battle-prone airplanes. A hasty slathering of herbal oils over sweaty limbs, and the little fighter planes hovered a decent distance away. The alligators rose once more to the surface, and sometimes nosed sneakily toward the canoe, curious but also hesitant with caution. The men never took Tara, the dog, with them, having been told she was fishing bait for alligators. People said that gators ate cats and dogs who were unwary.

On the river, as the mist lifted, the big birds settled back to fish in the shallows. Floating slowly homeward, the men passed through cypress forest, wet and ancient. Waterlily leaves hosted small jeweled frogs; and fish lips broke the surface whispering silent fish-thoughts. Life was all around, stirring aquatic. They were passing through Eden, sharing the first dawn.

When they reached the shore next to the trailer, they pulled the boat up and had a quick outdoor shower and a hasty breakfast. They worked with renewed appetite, brighter and broader, their minds feeling big enough to hold the river.

Marina rarely had time to come to Orange Blossom, but Chance went to see her several times a month. He would spend the day windsurfing and sometimes casually filming with a small hand held camera. He and Marina shared the nights, unfolding newly found places in their adult selves. Marina was mysterious in the depth of her womanhood. Chance thought he would never reach the end of who she was. On the other hand, she seemed to know him, and perhaps liked him better than he liked himself.

He regretted the lack of time she gave to him, but he knew that what he loved most in her came from her deeply intelligent and vibrant involvement in that which she cared about.

'Going Om' was finished just before Thanksgiving. Marina and Chance went back to Millertown for the holiday. Buddy met them at the door, looking more furrowed and time-gathered than Chance expected. When he saw Grace sitting in the cool dark parlor, he understood the story that had traced itself on Buddy's caring face.

Grace was a faded vision of herself. She smiled wanly from a chalky and weary face. The crow's-feet of pain and limitless fatigue spread from the corners of her eyes and mouth. She raised a listless hand, which Chance wrapped in both of his.

"I'm sorry you find me this way." she said with true regret.

Chance looked around at Marina to see if she had known that Grace was ill. The overwhelming grief he saw in her eyes told him this was new to her. He blinked back tears, not wanting to add one drop of pain to Grace's cup. Marina came and took her other hand, smiling sadly at her.

"Tell me all about yourselves." said Grace; her voice came from quite a distance inside her. It was hushed and a little breathless. "It's a good thing I have no news because I have no breath to tell it," she said with a tiny sliver of her old gaiety.

Buddy stood leaning in the doorway, ready to intervene against any shadows that might try to approach Grace.

Chance and Marina told her little bits of their doings, and she smiled and nodded softly, drinking in every word, warm through with the happiness of having them there with her.

Very soon she was too tired, and Buddy led Marina and Chance into the kitchen. The three sat at the kitchen table, painfully aware of Grace's empty chair.

"Why on earth didn't you tell us she was sick?" whispered Chance, trying not to raise a noise that would disturb Grace.

"We didn't think it would serve any purpose to worry you right now."

"Maybe we wanted to be worried." suggested Marina gently. "What's wrong with her? How worried should we be?"

"She's got a lung ailment. The doctors aren't sure what. She wouldn't let them look at her until she was really sick." The frustration and defeat in his voice caught both their attention.

Marina and Chance stayed for a week. The two of them made a beautiful Thanksgiving feast, under Grace's guidance. She sat at the kitchen table and cut out dough for dinner rolls, using an old pineapple can with both ends cut out. Chance and Marina had a million questions, wanting to make everything just exactly as Grace always had.

She smiled and said, "You know, you have to let your own spirit speak if you want to make something really fine. Just use my way as a framework, and feel a little bit free, make it your own; it will come out just fine."

It did come out just fine, but Chance and Marina both thought it was mainly because of all the little hints and details she gave them as they were cooking. While they were chopping celery and onions for the dressing, Grace said,

"I'm really worried about Buddy."

What's wrong with Buddy?" Chance worried now.

Grace answered, "He looks like a cross between a hot water heater with a stuck relief valve and a puff ball fungus that has deflated."

They couldn't help laughing; it was such an accurate description of the way he was looking. Then Grace continued, "He's hardly going to the garage at all. He's afraid to leave me alone here. He's been as kind as could be, looking after me- bless his heart- but he needs to be out, doing."

"There's always plenty to do around here." replied Chance, thinking of all the fence mending and hay pitching of his teen age years.

"I know," said Grace, "But he's not bringing in an income, and he's trying to hide that from me; but he's started stretching his dollars so far that they're going to have to be rewoven before the next person can use them. I wish you would have a talk with him. See if you can't ease his mind a little, so he'll go back to work some."

"We'll try." said Chance.

"But you know how stubborn he is!" added Marina.

The next day, Marina went out to the barn where Buddy was mending a harness. Chance stayed in the parlor with Grace and read 'Larkrise to Candleford' aloud to her, to her great delight.

Marina patted Kate, the black Belgian mare, on the nose while she and Buddy had a chat.

"I'm sorry we're only staying a week." she said, "You know if you want me here, I'll drop what I'm doing and come back home?"

"What and break your grandmother's heart? That's the last thing in this world that would make her happy. Don't you worry, we're making out just fine."

"It doesn't really seem like you are. Seems more like making do."

Buddy sat down on a bench and ran his hands through his hair, looking down at the ground. "Marina, I won't kid you-I feel like I'm borrowing from tomorrow just to keep today going. But I don't want you quitting school. It's your golden future and if you stop now you may never find your way back to it. Nope, this old mule can pull the sleigh a while longer. Just needed a little breather, and you and Chance have given me that."

"I do have an idea." said Marina. "I have a friend who might want to come live here and look after Grace while she's sick. He would do a wonderful job of it, if he'll come."

"I don't know," said Buddy dubiously. "I don't want anyone around who's going to put a strain on Grace. And besides, I couldn't pay your friend anything."

"He wouldn't take money if you offered it. As a matter of fact, he couldn't-he's a Buddhist monk."

"Is that right?" replied Buddy. "Is this the movie star monk?"

"The very one. I know you and Grace will really like him. And he would probably bring Tara, the chow dog. That way you could have a dog, but Ten Ha would take care of her. Tara would certainly brighten up Grace's life; and if Ten Ha works out, you could get back to the garage."

"I'm mighty tempted. " said Buddy. "What's the return policy on monks?"

"Satisfaction guaranteed or free shipping to send him back to us."

"Girl, it's good to have you back here!" he said as he gave her a hug.

Chance and Grace had been discussing the same solution and Grace was delighted with the idea.

"I don't know which I like better; orange monk or orange dog. We've wanted to have another dog, but Buddy was afraid it would be too much trouble for me. If Ten Ha will come, it would really take the pressure off Buddy. You don't know how it kills me to be such a weight to him!"

By the time the week was over, Grace had recovered enough strength to slowly make her way to the garden where she sat weeding and trimming the faded blossoms.

The day came to leave and they drove away with Buddy at the wheel of his old truck. Grace waved from inside the front screen door trying not to let a tear fall until they were out of sight.

On the way to the airport, Chance handed an envelope across Marina to Buddy, saying, "This is to help make sure Grace has everything she needs and all the care she needs to get well."

"We don't need your money." said Buddy, refusing to take the envelope.

Chance continued to lean across Marina, offering the money, "I know you don't need it, but I need to give it to you. I can't be here right now and I need to feel like I'm doing something to help out here. Please, take it! Shep and I hit a jackpot of money; we didn't do anything to earn it- it's silly noodle money."

Buddy took the envelope and stuffed it unopened into his shirt pocket. "I'll put it in the bank and we'll know it's there if we need it. I thank you for wanting to help out."

Chance wasn't quite satisfied with Buddy's answer, but he let it go. For now.

When they got to Florida, Marina and Chance went straight from the airport to the Buddhist temple. The monks were openly delighted to see them. Tara leaned happily against Marina's side, then against Chance's, then against Marina again. The dog grinned her purple-tongue smile.

Because Ten Ha would accept no money for his part in the movie, Shep and Chance had set up a scholarship fund for some of the Cambodian children in the community, with Ten Ha as administrator. This was a very popular move with the monks and with many of the Cambodians in the area. As soon as Chance came through the door of the temple, a small party was set in motion. Marina and Chance were put in ceremonial chairs and several women from the neighborhood appeared carrying steaming bowls of aromatic food. Marina and Chance knew that Ten Ha would not be sidetracked into any serious discussion until after the honorable occasion had been observed. Marina shrugged, and they settled back to enjoy themselves. Ten Ha declared,

"This is Cambodian Thanksgiving feast. Giving thanks for your kind sponsorship of our Cambodian children-boys and girls!"

Marina grinned. Shep had stipulated the scholarships had to be shared equally among both sexes, which was a novel concept in that community.

After about two hours of eating and many small impromptu speeches, the dishes were clear and Marina told

Ten Ha their proposal. He listened carefully until she finished speaking, and then said, "No problem."

Marina and Chance both leaned back, relieved.

Ten Ha said. "First, I have interviews with students- see that they are making progress, working very hard. Then I go care for your grandmother. Very good job for monk. Lu Kah, brother monk, will also be very happy-be big boss again. BUT," he put up his index finger, "you two must help Lu Kah make decisions about scholarship boys and girls. Lu Kah maybe have good hard mind, but maybe heart a little hard, too. I give you two each equal vote for decisions about the children. You come here, check one time a month, talk to children. See everything going in good direction."

"Gladly! It means I'll see Marina once a month."

"Good perk." said Ten Ha, smiling.

The monks stood in the yard bowing as they said goodbye.

'Going Om' was accepted as an entry in the Saltair Film Festival, which was held in February on the Connecticut River, near Mark and Marie's house. Before the festival, Marina and Chance drove home to Grace's for Christmas, bringing Ten Ha and Tara with them.

"I'll get Ten Ha's bags." said Buddy, as Chance and Marina brought their own suitcase and backpack into the hall.

"No need. No luggage." said Ten Ha.

"Real monks don't own anything." explained Chance.

"And artificial ones?" asked Buddy.

"Maybe own moon." answered Ten Ha.


Once the visitors had shaken off the road dust, Grace suggested that Tara be introduced to the chickens.

"Let's see if she's hunter or shepherd." said Buddy. "And I'll see which camp your friend here is in." nodding toward Ten Ha.

Ten Ha laughed and said, "A man can be both."

Chance and Marina went out to the backyard, Tara on a tightly held leash. They returned ten minutes later, to report that Tara was a sheep in wolf's clothing, lying down in the midst of the hens while they pecked around her toenails. They found Buddy seated on the sofa and Ten Ha lotused on an ottoman, in rapt conversation with each other about the best ways to keep cows contented and healthy.

Buddy told them, "Turns out Ten Ha here grew up on a farm. He says his home place looks pretty much like southern Florida. Cattle country with palm trees. He knows how to hand carve and assemble an ox cart. Maybe we'll build one while he's here, and get an ox to pull it. He says a lot of farmers in Cambodia use ox carts to get their produce to market." Buddy had not sounded this enthusiastic in quite a while.

"That's really great!" said Marina, "But did he pass your stringent test for nurse and companion for Grace?"

"Hell, anyone who takes as good a care of his cows as he does, has the best references I know."

Grace was dozing in her arm chair, feet up on a footstool, and a light blue blanket draped over her. She had been breathing with a shallow wheeze, but now she mooed softly and opened her eyes.

"May I examine her?" asked Ten Ha.

"Not very much of her, you can't!" said Buddy sharply.

"No, just her pulse, her tongue." Ten Ha reassured him. "Normally, monk not touch woman, but because Grace is sick, no problem-special situation. "

"What about food?" asked Chance. "How will you and Grace eat during the day."

"Also no problem. When no one can cook for monk, monk permitted to cook for ownself and sick persons. "

Grace stirred in her chair and said to Ten Ha, "Darlin', come on over and take my pulse."

He lifted her arm and laid three fingers across hers wrist. He pressed each finger , one at a time, into the flesh on her wrist. Then he did the same with her other wrist. He felt her cheek and looked at her tongue.

"Well?" asked Buddy

"Grace sick." said Ten Ha seriously. "Heart and lungs. Heart not beating big enough, lungs having water."

"Well said." said Buddy soberly. "That's pretty much what the doctors concluded. It took them about three weeks longer than you to figure that out. Got any ideas?"

"Yes. Grace should be happy. Good for her. I will try to help her be happy."

"That's a prescription I can live with!" said Grace.

"Yes." said Ten Ha.

Tara came and rested her marigold-colored head on Grace's thigh. Grace stroked the deep wool ruff around her neck, then said,

"Thank you. Thank you all. You've brought me just the friends I needed to help me get well again."


It was Ten Ha's first experience with Christmas. The tree delighted him. It had been a mild winter so far, and there were still some chrysanthemums, asters and marigolds blooming in Grace's garden. He picked most of them, and he and Grace strung garlands which he chanted over, and then hung them all over the tree.

Grace wasn't well enough to play the piano, so they sang carols acapello. Ten Ha found the songs very beautiful and strange. Marina and he preferred the ones about the animals in the manger, and the shepherds lying under the stars.

When Chance and Marina left, Ten Ha was already at home in Grace and Buddy's' hearts. The monk was deeply contented to be caring for Grace; he found her to be a sympathetic soul. The pleasure of being part of farming life again was also precious to him. To be involved in the rhythms of the turning of the sun, and the breathing of the domestic beasts, anchored his meditation once more in the gravity of the natural world.

January passed quietly for everyone. Mid-month, Buddy called Marina, to report that Grace was showing some signs of improvement, and was taking short walks with Ten Ha and Tara along the river. Buddy said he was working at the garage full time, and that after work he and Ten Ha were carving the pieces for an ox cart.

Chance, Shep and Sylvia went to Connecticut early in February. Marina could not take time off, although Chance pleaded with her. The three travelers stayed with Mark and Marie, on the wintery Long Island Sound. The world there looked like it was made of washed charcoal.

Sylvia dressed like an Eskimo and still said she didn't think she would ever be warm again. Marie tried to be cool and aloof from them, but quickly melted under the combined warmth and wit of Shep and Sylvia.

"Honey child, pass me the crackers, would you?" Sylvia said to Marie. Marie looked at her hard.

"If there is a honey child in this room, it's got to be you, Sylvia."

"I know what you mean." Shep chimed in. "I'm writing a song for her write now, entitled "My Honey Dipped Darling."

"Darling!" said Sylvia, her sweet voice coating the word.

Mark pronounced, "Your moniker in this house will have to be "Honey" from now on.

"Alright Sugar, I don't mind."

"A person could gain weight just being in the room with your language." Marie remarked.

Chance said, "Yeah, we have to limit her lines on the set. Some of the crew were getting pre-diabetic."

That evening, they were a jolly group as they entered the film house for the screening of 'Going Om'. As they walked down the aisle to their seats, Marie pointed out the critic for the New Yorker magazine, then the one for the Rolling Stone, and finally the New York Times critic. Shep and Chance each began to shrink a little inside.

"God! What if we bomb?" whispered Shep.

"Then it's going to be a mighty long walk back out of here." said Chance.

"Oh hush!" said Sylvia. "Who cares what a couple of baldheaded Yankees think?"

"An awful lot of theatre-goers care." answered Shep, sinking into his seat.

The film started and within five minutes, Chance and Shep were grinning at each other in the dim light from the screen. The audience was swept into the story, laughing large, weeping a little, and sometimes listening so intently that the silence in the theatre was palpable.

When the lights came up there was a roar of enthusiasm. Mark was beaming and Marie was stunned

"I knew you would make a good film. I never imagined you would do this!" She bent at the waist and said, "I bow to the new masters. And Honey, you are going to be gobbled up by Hollywood."

"Golden Girl!" said Shep proudly.

People were pressing around them, some of the crowd thrusting paper and pen at Sylvia.

"Autographs! Yes!" she cried enthusiastically. "Oh I love this!" as she signed. She whispered to Marie, "Do you think I might get to do the Miss America wave?"

A man came on the stage in front of the screen and spoke shrilly through a microphone, "People! Please! Please return to your seats. We have several more screenings to get through tonight."

No one paid any attention to him, although he continued to make similar announcements for the next hour. Several young men wanted to carry Shep and Chance around the theatre on their shoulders, but the directors demurred.

"Scared of heights." said Chance in a serious voice. "Both of us." Shep nodded gravely.

It took a long time for them to make their way to the door. Congratulations, handshakes, many photographs were taken of Sylvia. They found Mr. Bowden when they finally squeezed their way out to the sidewalk. He was ecstatic,

" This is a historic night for cinema. I can't believe I have been here to witness the birth of a land mark film!"

"Witness? You were the midwife, man!" said Shep.


Chance found the next few days disorienting and unreal. It felt like a dam of enthusiasm had broken, and was carrying them away in a massive surge. He called Marina the day after the screening. After congratulating him, she told him,

"Ten Ha is sure glad he's safe at Grace's house. Reporters, studio agents, kooks are swarming around the Buddhist temple here trying to co-opt a piece of Ten Ha or squee-gee some enlightenment off of him. Boon Ho is having a whale of a time. In fact all three monks are reveling in the attention. But, Ten Ha says he wants no part of this. He's insisting on maintaining his anonymity."

"Okay. Boy, I never imagined anything like this happening! We'll be careful not to let anyone know where he is or anything about him. It's just wild up here. So many people are trying to get in touch with Sylvia that it's jamming the phone lines in this town. Flowers are coming in the front door for her faster than Marie can ship them out the back door to the hospitals and nursing homes. Sylvia is loving it! But what a circus."

"When will you be coming back?"

"I'm not sure. There is going to be a screening in New York City next week, so sometime after that. Do you miss me?"

"I do."

"I always like to hear you say those words!"


That evening, he called her again.

"I wish you would reconsider and come up here this weekend. 'Going Om' is being given a special showing at the Clinton Theatre in Manhattan; and immediately after there will be the premier of 'A Studied Woman', that documentary I made of Victoria. Then, a huge reception full of fabulously famous people. I really want you with me; this is IT-the celebration of my success!"

"Alright, I'll see if I can get on a plane and come for the weekend." Marina replied. Chance whooped with delight.

Marina was at a critical place in her field studies, many of the young birds and mammals were just out of the nest and displaying hitherto unrecorded behaviors and interactions. Her professor was not happy with her leaving. He told her she was going to have to be more serious about her commitment to her work, if she planned to excel in her studies. She apologized and got on a plane.

Chance collected her at the airport on Friday afternoon. On the way to Mark's house they stopped by the boatyard where the Spinthrift was cradled for the winter. They climbed a ladder and crawled under the tarp at her stern. Chance slid the hatch cover open and took Marina below. He pulled a sleeping bag from a locker and spread it on the rust colored cushions on the bunk. It was cold enough that they could see their breath, but when he laid Marina down and undid the top button of her blouse, her skin was flushed and as pink as a sun-warmed peach. He hastily pulled the sleeping bag over them and kissed her fiercely-held her so tight she gasped. She answered his powerful need with hers, and they moved hungrily, almost desperately, reaching for each other and trying to scale the tension, wanting it tauter and tauter until the flood of release-their minds and bodies going to liquid. Marina floated in the afterglow, while Chance jumped up, invigorated and ready to grab the world. Within two minutes, the sweat on both of them became icy and their teeth began to chatter. They hurried to rebutton, tuck, and smooth, and then climbed down the ladder with numbing fingers and rosy cheeks. They slammed the car doors shut, and Chance started the engine and the heater. They were shaking with cold and glee. As the air in the car heated, Marina felt the warm blood going back into her nose and her toes.

She looked at Chance and said, "I needed that!"

He grinned and reached over to hold her close and warm.

They arrived at Mark's looking like bright winter spirits, bringing icy air and light hearted gaiety into the hallway with them. Sylvia leapt from the sofa by the fireplace and ran to embrace Marina.

"You angel, you! Now the party can begin! Here's your hostess-my darling friend, Marie. She's a bit of a stick at first, but you just give her some sugar and she'll eat out of your hand!"

"Really!" snorted Marie.

"Watch her hind feet though, she's mighty uppity." Sylvia told Marina.

Mark overheard and said, "Don't worry, I hear Marina is studying animal behavior, she'll know how to calm a Ruffled Red-Faced Hostess."

"The way Marie is looking at you," said Sylvia said to Mark, "you'd best be studying animal bejabbers!"

Marie shook her head and said, "Welcome!" extending her hand to Marina. The two women took to one other immediately. Still holding Marie's hand, Marina looked around at her; the hallway and the rooms beyond were full of flowers. Marie and Sylvia had taken apart the bouquets and arranged massive floral arrangements everywhere.

"It looks like Titania's bower!" exclaimed Marina.

"Smells like heaven, too." sighed Sylvia, wrinkling her nose. "Helps keep those icicles out there at bay."

Marina was up and out at dawn, poking along the cold rocky shore in front of the house. The tide was out and she slipped and slithered over glowing orange-brown seaweed made of bumpy bladders filled with clear jelly. Little crabs scuttled away when she crouched down and lifted some of the plant heap from the round chocolate-brown rocks. In tide pools, small patches of vibrant green fluff and pale pink sea-lichen completed an unexpectedly vivid scene in miniature; hiding in the crannies of a bleak winter landscape. Several seals popped their heads above water and regarded her with liquid eyed curiosity, as she in turn examined this intertidal world she had never seen before.

One seal barked to her, sounding like a dog. Three seals swam closer to the shore, and hefted themselves onto a flat rock ten feet from where she squatted.

She spoke to them softly, " Hello there, how are you?"

The seals made quiet barking noises, nodding and twisting their heads. They sniffed hard in her direction and began inching their way across the rock, coming closer to her. She sat down gracefully and gently on a less-than-flat rock, barnacles scrapping at her thighs through her pants.

She said, "You look wonderful, my friends. I'm so glad to have you near me."

At this, the seals came right around her and bumped her gently with their noses. One slapped her lightly with his front flipper. They slipped and slid around her in a light hearted awkward dance. Suddenly one raised his head and froze in place. He yipped a warning and the three seals galumphed rapidly to the edge of the water, then slid like liquid into the sea. Marina looked around and saw Sylvia approaching, holding two steaming cups of coffee. Sylvia was bundled from her quilted booted feet to her Tibetan-jacketed and hooded head, her face framed in faux fur.

"I wanted to come out and have a real good girl-talk with you, but it's so cold my intentions have frozen. Anyway, I brought you some coffee."

"Thanks." said Marina, getting up from her awkward seat. They slid and stumbled back across the slicky rocks, then hurried across the frost rimed lawn to the warmth of the house. After divesting herself of her Arctic layers, Sylvia rushed to her usual spot on the sofa and wrapped a blanket around her shoulders.

"Come snuggle with me." she patted a cushion next to her. Marina came over and curled into the blanket with Sylvia. They talked softly and confidentially, giggles bubbling quietly up and low murmurings of sympathetic feeling. Mark came sock-footed, silent, down the stairs and stopped before entering the room, admiring the two pretty faces lit with friendship and the early morning light streaming through the window, coffee steaming in their cups.

The rest of the household was stirring, arriving in the breakfast room and milling sleepy-eyed and yawning, coming to terms with their own waking minds. After breakfast, people lingered at the table chatting about all the possibilities that were opening up for the two young directors.

Mark said, "You really need to get yourselves a business agent and advisor. Someone to handle all the ins and out, legalities, legitimacy of various deals. Someone to look after your interests so you can focus on your work."

"That's a good idea." said Chance.

"I can ask around, find out who's good in the business." offered Mark.

Chance asked Marie, "What would you think of taking the job?"

"Me?" said Marie, astounded.

Shep and Chance nodded at her, Mark looked at her thoughtfully. "It's not a bad idea." he said.

"What do I know about the movie business?"

"You're a natural, my girl." said Mark.

Chance joined in, "You're smart, tough, insightful, energetic."

"I do have a law degree," said Marie, "although I've never used it. But surely you should get someone with experience!"

"I don't think so." said Chance, "I think you would be more than a match for any two-bit movie shyster that comes along. And you'll have our interests at heart, we'll be able to concentrate on making movies."

Mark said, "I don't think anyone in this room wants to get entangled in commercial movie production. Marie, you might enjoy doing battle to keep these guys a maverick operation. It will certainly be a challenge to out-maneuver the professional two-legged rats that are already coming out of the woodwork.

Marie said she would do a little research and let them know in a day or two. "In the meantime, don't sign ANYTHING or verbally agree to ANYTHING. If a waiter asks you if you want extra mayo on that burger, say "no" until you've talked to me."

"What about me?" asked Sylvia, "You're not going to leave me out here on my own, are you?"

Marie replied, "Your career is going to make some agent ridiculously wealthy and prematurely grey. You are going to have to find someone who will handle you full time."

"Where am I supposed to find this someone? This devotee with immense talent and integrity?" asked Sylvia skeptically.

Mark said, "For now, follow the advice Marie just gave to Shep. Don't sign or agree to anything. I'll ask around in the city and see if I can find an agent for you temporarily. You know, you'll probably be out in Hollywood. I don't know if it makes a difference, you may want an agent who's located there."

Shep and Sylvia looked at each other in dismay.

"I don't want to be in Hollywood!" wailed Sylvia.

"There, there!" Shep put his arm around her. "No one is going to force you to be a mega Hollywood star if you don't want to be."

Everyone laughed, getting up from the table to go their separate ways, to get ready for the evening of glitter and fame.

Arriving at the theatre, they walked the cordoned way from curbside to entrance, cameras flashing, reporters shouting rapid-fire questions at Sylvia. The press was grasping talon-like onto her expected fame, trying to hoist her overhead into view, hungry for 'the now-the new'. They were caught up in their own excitement of creating a myth. Sylvia strolled through the throng, sublime and relaxed. The velvet cordon rope created a magical aisle of peace. She smiled sweetly at every thrusting face. She seemed to be simultaneously available and out of reach. As she gained the steps of the theatre, she turned back and said softly, "I appreciate your enthusiasm and I'm grateful. I hope, after you have seen this movie, you will also have found some modicum of pleasure in the acting we have put before you."

The reporters cheered her and shouted. When she got inside the lobby, she shook her head.

Shep said, "You have those beasts eating out of your hand! How can you be so patient with their shoving and shouting and rudeness?"

"Honey, they mean well, they just don't know any better."

"I don't think they mean well at all." said Shep.

"No they probably don't, but that attitude will carry you far." observed Mark to Sylvia.


They settled back into their seats and watched the film, basking in the audience response. When the film ended, Shep, Chance, and especially Sylvia were lionized all the way to the bar in the lobby. Everyone wanted to touch them. Women in glittering jewels, coiffed to a degree of elegance that was frightening, tried to catch a crumb of conversation. Some of Mark's colleagues rode on his acquaintance to get close enough to be photographed next to the film makers. Marina tried to escape the pressing crowd but Chance held her elbow tightly. He smiled and chatted easily with anyone who addressed him. Shep joked, or listened quietly to the many things that people were intent on telling him. Chance spoke in Marina's ear,

"Don't slip away-this is my moment of glory. I want to share it with you."

"Your film is the glory." she whispered back. "You don't need me here, let me go have a quiet drink at the bar and admire all your admirers from afar."

He let her go and turned back to the two tuxedoed men who were asking him if he knew such-and-such very important person. When he answered in the negative, they assured him with great assurance that he would need to know such-and-such in order to go forward in his career. They were shoved aside by a determined bejeweled matron who said they simply must come to lunch on Tuesday, just an intimate gathering of sixty or seventy people. Before

Chance could answer, she too was swept away by the pressure of importance swelling impatiently behind her.

The lights flickered and the theatre goers flowed back to their seats, rustling and flashing as they went.

'A Studied Woman' played to an almost silent house. The movie was an hour long, tight and pure. Victoria's voice: hard, desirable, ruthless-cut through the air. In the film she was completely free of inhibition, seemingly unaware that the camera was filming. And yet, she was playing to the lens, unembarrassedly exposing her own selfish, cold, grasping nature. It was an extraordinary display of almost naïve trust in the camera man's insignificance-an intimacy with the camera in which she exposes the calculating artifice she uses to dupe the world. Chance's choice of black and white film brought an odd luminosity to her beauty at certain times, making her seem almost mythical. In the last scene, Victoria is applying makeup skillfully-like an artist, enhancing every attribute, minimizing every flaw and creating the illusion of wearing almost no makeup at all. The film fades as she looks into the mirror with satisfaction and pleasure at her finished face.

There was silence in the theatre, then applause began to ripple, growing as the grip of the film loosened on the watchers. People stood and began to call for the director. Chance stood and bowed as the applause continued. Finally people began to leave their seats and once more Chance and his friends were surrounded in the foyer. Chance asked Marina what she thought; she had not seen the movie previously.

She said, 'I think it would have been better to leave it unseen."

Chance was shocked and surprised by her answer. "You heard the applause, it's a really good film."

"It surely is," she said, "but it's a violation of the trust that woman placed in you. A woman that you loved. How could you?"

She wriggled away from him and disappeared into the crowd. He looked after her, lost and confused by her reaction. He turned to Shep, who had overheard the quarrel, then remembered Shep had advised him to keep the movie in the can.

Shep said, "Here comes trouble," as the crowd parted and Victoria stepped through. She looked white-faced and slightly dispossessed.

"All hail the conquering film maker! You certainly got the last word!"

"Hello Victoria, how are you?" asked Chance.

"Ruined, thanks to you!" Chance noticed Jack Evans, the senator, was accompanying her. Cameras were snapping as she leaned toward Chance.

"I would never have expected this kind of cruelty from you. I didn't think you had it in you." It was difficult to know if she was praising or damning him.

"I didn't make it to be cruel." answered Chance.

"No, you made it to be famous." she said, laughing bitterly. "I can understand that."

Senator Evans nodded to Chance and said to Victoria, "Dear, perhaps we should be going, the Press is coming this way."

"Too late." said Shep. The cameras surrounded Victoria, again reporters shouted out rude or inflammatory questions. Victoria said to them disdainfully,

"No need to pour gasoline on a fire."

"So you must be really angry about this expose! Are you going to sue?"

"How does it feel to be the Dark Queen of Documentary?"

Victoria turned to face her tormentors. "It feels archetypal. It's a case of the good," she pointed to the area of room where Sylvia was holding court, "the bad," she pointed to herself, "and the ugly," pointing to Chance.

    The reporters laughed and scribbled. Chance edged away from Victoria; half the reporters stayed with her, surprised at her wit and admiring her silver steeliness. The senator looked like he was considering whether discretion in the form of desertion could possibly construed as the better part of valor. In his final analysis it seemed that an obsession with Victoria's immense charisma was the strongest force within him, and he stayed by her side, married and senatorial though he was.

    Gradually the crowd moved out through the doors into the night, cold and neon. Limousines and cabs carried the fortunate to the penthouse reception. The fete was an exhausting round of accolades and celebration. The novelty of southern celebrity was offensive and unavoidable. Sylvia handled the Lilliputians of Manhattan magnanimously. She stepped with generosity around their embarrassing potholes of cultural ignorance and prejudice. Once again, Shep admired her immense social aplomb.

    "Oh Honey, they're just small town folks with a big town backdrop." she explained to him."You be just as kind and tolerant as you were to all of us in Orange Blossom, and you' all get along just fine." She patted him on the knee, her eyes twinkling wickedly.

    At two in the morning, Marie, the unofficial manager, told them it would be alright to leave. They went to Mark's uptown apartment and all six of them found some place to lay their weary heads for an exhausted few hours of sleep.

    The next day was Sunday. Marina was flying home that evening, so while everyone else went back to Connecticut, Chance and Marina stayed in the city for the day. When they were alone in the apartment at last, Chance tried to heal the rift that Victoria's film had created.

"As I told Victoria last night, I didn't make the film to be cruel."

"That's like saying if you run over a dog because you were driving recklessly, it's alright, because you didn't mean to run over the dog!"

"Victoria is not a helpless dog who happens to be in the road."

"No, she's a vicious beautiful dog who happens to be in the road." said Marina. "She trusted you when she let you film her. And you edited that footage after you two broke up. You edited with a completely different view of her than you had when you were filming."

"I can't believe you are defending Victoria!" shouted Chance, exasperated and frustrated.

"It's not Victoria I'm concerned about." said Marina. "She can obviously take care of herself. It's you that worries me."

"Me?" exclaimed Chance, unbelieving. "Me! It's my art! That's what I do! I make movies. That is a great movie. It's beautiful, it's true, it's complex, it's intriguing."

"It's cruel, it's disloyal, it's dishonorable!" shouted Marina back at him.

Chance said, "I really cannot believe your take on this. Is this how you support me as an artist?"

"And I can't believe you can be this cold-natured." responded Marina. "I didn't know this part of you existed. I thought I knew you so well. Where did this come from?"

"It's my art! My films are who I am. They are everything to me. Am I not supposed to make the best film I possibly can. Am I supposed to not create what might offend?"

"Of course not," said Marina. "I am astonished at how blind you are being to what is wrong here."

"I sure can't see it." said Chance crossly. "I guess we are going to have to agree to disagree."

Marina looked at him sadly and said, "I guess we will."

"So do you still love me?" he asked.

She smiled at him sadly and said, "I will always love you."

"From some patronizing moral high ground?" he asked, less angry now.

"If need be." she answered.

"Well. Will you consider lowering a rope sometimes?"

"Sure, if you can catch the other end of it!"

She came into his arms and they made love. For the first time, their passion contained a trace of sadness. The distance between their hearts had poignancy, somehow deepening the feelings they had for each other physically. As if they were nostalgic for some small lost intimacy between their souls.

Chance put her on the plane, watching her light-footed step, her beloved back disappear into the unknown future.

When Marie got back to Connecticut, she formally accepted the position of business manager for Spanish Moss Productions, with the caveat that she worked from home or New York. Documents were signed, the business was official, and Shep, Sylvia and Chance went home to Orange Blossom.

They found Sylvia's great-aunt, Margaret, exhausted. Strangers had besieged her house, badgering her beyond her endurance. Some were agents for Hollywood production companies trying to stake out claims to Sylvia's career; others were employees of what Miss Margaret called 'Scandal Sheets'.

"I cannot dignify them with the term 'reporter'." she exclaimed. "They have asked me the most degraded and sordid questions imaginable. If James hadn't come to the rescue, I believe you would have come home to nothing but a dried out old mummy, sucked dry by those rascals."

She was speaking of James Mullican, who played the doctor in 'Going Om'. When he heard that strangers were swarming Miss Margaret's porch, he came immediately. Before he was through the gate, eight individuals came clamoring down the porch steps. Two of them thrust papers under his nose, one of them saying, 'Here's your contract-right here-best offer-just go on and sign it. I'll explain the terms to you later."

James waved his arms slowly, as if he were wading through a crowd of hungry cows, his dignified bearing highlighting their untoward behavior. When Miss Margaret heard his voice, she came to the door and unhooked the latch to let him in.

"You'll never know how relieved I am to see you. I've been practically marooned here, it's such a gauntlet one must run, to leave the house."

"I think the sheriff will send a few deputies and clear this mess off, if you call him."

"Then I'll have to entertain the deputies, getting them lemonade and cookies day and night. I wish those movie makers would hurry up and come home. They created this problem. It's hard enough that they took Sylvia off, without sending this pack of vermin down on our heads!"

He went back to the porch and Miss Margaret smiled to herself as she heard him talk to the men outside. It sounded like Moses driving the Philistines from her door, complete with thunder and echoes of the voice of God. The besiegers actually ran down the steps and jostled at the gate, except one, who returned up the stairs, saying, "Here's that contract I was trying to tell you about. This is your ticket out of this tiny tedious town."

James, answering in his normal speaking voice, velvet as young moss, said, "Send it to my agent, here is his card."


James was very glad to be relieved of guard duty, telling Shep, "I've been signed to play Hamlet in a production to be filmed in Venice. I'm going to need every minute to prepare for the role. I've been reading Shakespeare's plays to myself, all of my life, but I've never tried to speak the lines."

"Venice, eh?" said Shep thoughtfully. "I haven't mentioned this to Chance or Sylvia, but I've been turning an idea over in my head about the next film. I'm toying around with a romantic comedy starring you and Sylvia.

Venice might be a good setting. It seems like that city is always a major character in every movie filmed there."

"I don't think I can make two movies at the same time." answered James. "I'm as grateful as I can be for the opportunity you gave me in 'Going Om' and I'll be happy to do another movie with you and Chance, but an opportunity to play Hamlet means more to me than I can tell you. Especially this production: it's got a brilliant cast and it will be straight up Shakespearian drama, no clever modern twists."

"How long do they expect filming to run?"

"April and May."

"What if we planned to start production after that?"

"That would be a definite possibility." said James. "But don't you think I'm rather old to play Sylvia's love interest? And, I don't really want to make a race movie."

"I'm planning to write this script specifically for Sylvia and you- you aren't too old. The part will be for a man your age. I'm planning to have the story be light and funny about two very different characters overcoming various misunderstandings, to find the true course of love. A little 'As You like It', a little Austen, and a lot of Shep and Chance."

"And a lot like a race movie!"

"No. I think placing the film abroad will hopefully allow the characters to be two humans in love, above everything else. The major difference may be age, or gender, or possibly culture."

"I'll look at the script and we'll see." James finished the conversation.


Everyone at Spanish Moss, except Miss Margaret, embraced Shep's idea with great enthusiasm. For Sylvia it meant resuming the normal rhythms of life with her great aunt, with Shep being at home writing the script. For

Chance it meant an opportunity to spend more time with Marina, and time to explore the swampy wilds around Orange Blossom; a restorative that would recharge his creative juices.

'Going Om' was the surprise smash hit of the year, taking mainstream America by storm. Marie proved to be supremely talented at the business of business. She exulted in the whole energetic melee of it and filled the coffers of Spanish Moss to the point of bursting.

"Venice?" she said when she heard the proposal. "Venice is much too expensive to film in! There are some other islands nearby that will do just as well, for one tenth the cost. You can film a little grandiose footage at the Doge's palace, and that will be all we need in Venice proper."

"How do you know these things?" asked Chance, astonished.

"I've read things here and there." she said.

Over the next two weeks, Shep wrote relentlessly, hour after hour. When he had a first draft completed, he invited James, Chance, Sylvia and Miss Margaret to a reading. It was a lovely story: light, loving, comical. Miss Margaret was the first to comment,

"You can't make that into a movie, not if you want to remain welcome in this town."

"I'm afraid I agree." added James. "All of my family and all of my wife's family live around here. They would never be safe again. I would have to move Louise and the children someplace far away."

Shep at first was crestfallen. "Oh come on, it's not that radical."

Chance said, "It will make a good movie, especially set in Venice. And besides, I thought we wanted to push the limits, break some new ground with our films."

"I doubt James wants to be martyred for the sake of a fluffy love comedy." said Miss Margaret, dryly. "And maybe Sylvia doesn't want to sacrifice the possibility of a Hollywood career over a load of light piffle."

Shep bridled a little. "It's really good light piffle," he said, "Fluffy, bubbly."

"Black cream." countered Miss Margaret.

"They don't do more than kiss." observed Chance.

Sylvia had been silent until now. "It's a charming script, and a wonderful role for James and me. I will be delighted to do it. But," she added thoughtfully, "I don't want to put James and his family into any danger."

"I cannot do it." said James. "I cannot risk the harm this could do to my family; the unhappiness it could bring. And, I don't want to jeopardize my opportunity at a career in film. I've been a farmer all my life, living in a world of dreams and books at night. I can't throw it all away for this one movie. I know I owe you a world of gratitude," he said to Chance and Shep. "I wouldn't ever have come to the attention of the world without you, and being in 'Going Om' is the most fulfilling experience I've ever had. But I cannot oblige you in this matter. I'm terribly sorry."

Shep was still not ready to yield. Chance half-heartedly supported him in his efforts to sway James and Miss Margaret.

Finally Miss Margaret said in exasperation, "Shep, you are from Ohio. You don't understand the hornet's nest you are about to poke a stick into. And both of you are too young and green to know about the suffering this particular hornet's nest can bring. A man has to choose his fights wisely, particularly a black man in this neck of the woods. I think James probably has more courage in his little finger than either of you will ever have in your whole lives; but thank God he also has more sense than the two of you young fools will ever need! Now stop badgering the man, apologize to him for your thoughtlessness and be grateful none of us will have to suffer the dose of reality you were attempting to bring down on us."

Shep looked at her in shock but Chance quickly said, "Yes ma'am! James, I'm sorry I didn't think this out more clearly. I got caught up in the possibilities in the film, and lost sight of what it might mean in your life, and in Sylvia's, for that matter."

James was relieved. "You can easily cast a white man in that role and still have a very good film. As you said, Shep, it's not really a race related story."

Shep was disappointed. "That part was written for you, no one else is going to be able to do it justice."

Miss Margaret went to sleep that night feeling that tranquility had been restored. James and his wife felt a menace recede like the shadow of a demon ebbing away from their doorway.

Chance, Shep and Sylvia sat up discussing and arguing, the two young men impatient with the caution of their elders.

With no movie in the works, Chance decided to take time off, and went to stay with Marina. They camped in her patch of swamp and he filmed her with the animals she was observing. When she was in class, he spent a lot of time canoeing and wind surfing. Most mornings he swam for an hour in the cold winter southern sea, chilled despite the wet suit he wore.

In March he was permitted, as a volunteer camera man, to go along on a two week sea cruise, south of the Keys, where he and Marina dove and frolicked in the big winter waves. Marina was being drawn ever deeper into her studies of the animal world. It was a world she loved intensely and Chance felt fortunate that she had intensity enough left for her feelings for him. And that she did not find the two passions mutually exclusive. She was always glad to have him along in her explorations.

In Orange Blossom, James continued to prepare for his coming role while his wife, Louise, tried to pack what they might need for months abroad in a land she knew nothing about. And they both worked out arrangements for the care of their four older children, who were remaining in Orange Grove; it being decided that junior and senior high education should not be disrupted. The two younger children would accompany their parents to Venice.

Sylvia's new agent in Los Angeles sent her an offer that she accepted. She would costar with one of America's most popular young actors in a western adventure film. Shep went with her, to her immense relief. And Miss Margaret decided to go as well. "I plan to encamp upon the porches of several recent acquaintances and bedevil them in their homes to the same extent they bedeviled me in mine, while you-all were gone up North."

In April, Marina received a letter from Ten Ha:

Dear Marina and Chance,
Maybe you would like to come home for a little while and spend time with Grace. I think it might benefit you, and make you happy now and later. Grace is a wise woman, and sometimes it is good to drink from the cup when it is there for you. I continue to feel fortunate to be here with Grace and Buddy.
      Your Friend,
      Ten Ha

Marina said to Chance, "I think we should load up the car and go."

"What about your classes? The field study?"

"I can take a few days off. I think we should go, tomorrow."

"Do you think he means Grace has gotten sicker."

"I'm not sure. But I think he's right, we will be glad all our lives for the time we got to spend with Mimi. I want to see her. I'll make up the work I miss. And get someone to cover for me for a few days at the swamp."

When they spoke to Buddy on the phone that night, they could feel a dam break in his voice.

"We'll be mighty glad to see you. I know how busy you are, but I won't lie, we've been missing you something fierce."

They were home by the next night. Tara, the orange fur ball, bounced like a tennis ball on a clay court, filled with more joy than she could contain or express. Finally she ran madly around the house three times, an orange blur shooting past like a comet. Buddy and Ten Ha stood on the porch, blue jeans and benevolence looking down at Marina and Chance, as they entered through the magnificent flowers that sprawled everywhere inside the white picket fence.

"Grace and Ten Ha dropped a floral bomb in your honor." said Buddy, as he hugged Marina tight in his arms. Ten Ha bowed to them, wearing a warm smile all the way up to his brown eyes.

They entered the dim light of the parlor and saw Grace lying on the settee, propped up with pillows. She was so pale and wasted, Chance caught his breath. She smiled and lifted a feeble hand.

He went and knelt by her side, then laid his head on her thigh.

"Oh Gracie." he sounded forlorn and lost.

"Now, now. Do I look as bad as all that?" She spoke in a hush, but the glimmer of sweet laughter was still there.

"No, of course you don't!" answered Buddy. "You look beautiful."

And she did. Beautiful and fading.

"Yes," said Marina, "You look beautiful. But, tired."

"I am tired. I'm sorry not to get up to greet you, but Buddy and Ten Ha insisted that I stay on the sofa."

Ten Ha told them, "Today is one of the energy not too much days. Tomorrow maybe have energy too much, and she will help me in garden."

Buddy nodded and said, "She has plenty of good days."

Chance, still sitting on floor by her side said, "You look ethereal."

"Why thank you honey, you have not lost your gift for charming compliments, I see."

He laid his head upon her leg again and sighed, content to be with the one who had saved him and held his soul yet, in her keeping.

She looked at Marina and said, "Come give your Mimi a hug."

Marina bent down and gently wrapped her strong young arms around Grace's frail birdlike body, wishing she could infuse her own vitality into this cherished woman. Tara came and leaned against Marina, looking up at her and grunted very softly, as if to say she would add her vibrant strength as well.


Grace was well enough the next day to fix a dinner which brought back memories for everyone around the table. Buddy rested in the moment of recaptured happiness. A family again, for a little while. Ten Ha was a welcome part of the whole. Chance leaned back in his chair, tipping up the front legs. He hooked his thumbs through his belt loops and grinned at Grace. She thought he looked like the boy Marina brought home from the river, many years ago.

Buddy and Chance went out to the barn to tinker with the timing on the tractor, and Grace settled gratefully onto the settee in the parlour. Marina sat in the rocker next to her.

"You're tired!" said Marina softly, noting the quiet gurgling sound that was now ever-present in Grace's breathing.

"I'm always tired." answered Grace, without a trace of complaint in her voice. "Having you here gives me new life."

"Then I'll come more often."

"No, no! I didn't mean that! You need to keep focused on your studies-don't let anything distract you. You've got places to go, darling; and what I want most in life is to see you get there!"

"Chance is anxious for us to get married." said Marina.

"Put him off a while, girl." Grace's voice was gentle.

"I know I need to finish school."

"Yes you do!" Now Grace spoke more firmly. Marina looked over at her. Grace didn't often speak that way. Grace looked at her steadily; Marina thought maybe even sternly. Grace said nothing more so Marina let it drop.

Chance and Marina stayed two more happy days, then returned to Florida. On the drive home, Marina announced,

"I've decided to take the summer off from school."

"That's great, honey! We can get married and you can come to Italy with me. We'll honeymoon while Shep and I are working on the film."

"No. I want to spend the summer at home with Mimi and Buddy."

"Why?"

"Because Mimi is really sick and I want to be with her."

"Buddy and Ten Ha have that covered. You don't need to go."

"It's not a matter of need, in the practical sense. Grace needs me to be part of her life right now."

"Now I know Grace did not tell you that!" Chance exclaimed. "She's forever reminding me how important it is that you concentrate on your school work!"

"She doesn't have to tell me." answered Marina. "My heart tells me."

"What about me? What does your heart tell you about me?"

"My heart tells me I will love you forever."

"Forever is great, but what about now. What if I need you now?"

"But you don't." said Marina. "And anyhow, why don't you spend the summer at home, as well? We would be together, and be with Buddy and Mimi."

"That would be real nice," said Chance impatiently, "but you know I can't just give up my work. I've got a movie to make. Frankly, I'm surprised you're even considering dropping the ball with your research."

"You know how important that study is to me. Can't you understand that Mimi and Buddy need to come first now? Chance, they aren't going to be around forever, always available when you can fit them in."

"Oh come on, Grace is not that sick! She's just tired mostly and run down. "

Marina looked at him in disbelief. "Grace has congestive heart failure-it's carrying her down."

"I don't think it's as drastic as you're making it out to be. She'll be with us a good long while yet."

"That may well be, but I'm spending the summer with them!"

Chance changed the subject and they parted sweetly when he dropped her off at her apartment a few hours later.

In June, Marina went home to Grace and Buddy. Chance went to Italy, and Shep and Sylvia joined him on an island near Venice. James Mullican, having finished working in the Hamlet production, also joined them along with his wife, Louise, and two of their children. While Shep and Chance tussled with re-writing the script, Sylvia and the Mullican family began an earnest attempt to see every sight within a day's reach of the little island.

One day, Chance said, "What if the love story is in the past? What if a beloved woman has died? Maybe James' character is a bereaved widower here on some sort of pilgrimage. Either revisiting a place of memories, or seeing an iconic work of art. Maybe a painting that had been significant to his dead wife."

"That's not bad!" Shep said. "Could he encounter Sylvia's character in some deeply meaningful but unromantic way? James and Sylvia are going to have fabulous chemistry on the screen. And you know, being from the same town in real life, knowing each other all their lives while living in totally different circumstances- we ought to be able to pull off some real magic with what we've got to work with."

"It would get us around that interracial tangle, although I hate that we have to bend to that.. But you know, they're right. There is too much risk involved for James and Sylvia."

"I guess so." Shep was still not totally convinced. Then he shrugged and added, "Let's work on this new angle for a while and see what we come up with."

As they were working, Sylvia and the Mullican family visited the Academy of Art in Venice. The children wandered ahead while the adults lingered at certain paintings, impressed in the presence of the renaissance masters. The children came scampering quietly back and little Jennette pulled on her mother's hand.

"Mama," the eight year old whispered loudly, "There's a picture of Sylvia here."

Billy added, "Yeah, if she was a popsicle!"

"What?" Sylvia giggled. "If I was a popsicle! I didn't know they had any Warhol's here."

The children lead them through a series of galleries and they stood in front of a canvas on loan from another museum. It was a work by DaVinci and there in a supporting cast of angels was Sylvia, looking indeed as if she had been dipped in ice, emotionally.

Jennette said, "See, it's Sylvia. Only it's not Sylvia because Sylvia is like sunshine and that angel is not!"

"This is eerie." said Sylvia, feeling quite spooked to be staring at her own face across several centuries.

"Maybe the model is an ancestor of yours." suggested James.

"As far as I know, I don't have any Italian ancestors."

"The resemblance is really uncanny." James commented as he looked more closely at the painting.


Shep went to see the painting, the next day. He came home smiling widely. He entered the house and chucked Billy under the chin.

"You've made a great discovery." He did a little dance then clicked his heels together in the air. "This is going to help our script tremendously. "

He and Chance spent the afternoon sequestered in the logia. When they emerged in the evening, Chance announced to the household that they had nailed the plot.

"James' character's wife, love of his life, dies, and he is unable to overcome his grief. A copy of the DaVinci picture has been hanging over the mantle all their married life. It's been some kind of touchstone for her in all kinds of troubles and triumphs. James come to Italy to see the original, hoping he will connect with her spirit in some way, or at least have made a pilgrimage to see what she would have loved to see. It's lucky for us the painting is on loan here in Venice. Makes it easy to set the film here.

So, he sees Sylvia across one of the canals and recognizes her as one of the angels in the painting. He chases her, and she goes into Santa Maria della Salute, and when he gets there, she is gone. He encounters her and she eludes him again and again. It will make a nice tour of Venice, with each setting having a feeling of being heavily significant, but what the significance is will be mysterious until the end of the movie. The course of his pursuit will cause him to have several experiences that help him finally through the darkness of his grief. In the end he'll have a conversation with her-and she really will be an angel, sent to help him find his way back to life."

James spoke first, "It doesn't seem like much of a part for Sylvia."

"That's okay." she said, "It's a beautiful story."

Shep answered, "As he pursues her, he can witness various vignettes of her world-we don't quite have that worked out yet. So, what do you think?"

"Wonderful!" smiled Sylvia.

"Fantastic!" agreed James.

Shep added, "We're going to try to illuminate the relationship in the marriage, probably by mirroring scenes between men and women, that James witnesses while he is in Venice. It's kind of tricky and complicated, but if we can pull it off it will be sensational."

"And the city!" raved Chance. "What a city to film in! The light! The reflections! The colors! Who needs a plot?"

He and Shep settled in to write the complete script. Fired with enthusiasm, the days peeled by.

At home meanwhile, Marina was moving slowly through the summer heat. Grace spent most of her time sitting on the couch reading. Or more often the book would drop softly into her lap as she gazed out onto the flowered world that Ten Ha tended for her. Her smile was dreamy, in spite of the effort her lungs were making; struggling to pull each breath of air through the ocean of liquid accumulating in her lungs.

Buddy and Marina tended her as though she, too, was a garden of rare and fleeting flowers. One day as Buddy sat by her side holding her hand, she said,

"Sweetheart, I'm worried about you."

"There's no need to that, love." he said, and he kissed her cool forehead.

"I'm worried how you'll do after I'm gone."

"Don't say that, Grace!" Anguish broke almost silently, somewhere behind his voice.

"Oh love, you know it's true. I won't be here much longer and I'm worried how you'll get on when I'm not here anymore."

"I don't know how I'll do." he said at last. "I do know I am drinking in every second of time we have now, and I will hold you here as long as I can. I am not going to think about anything but this time we have now." He spoke with a gentle fierceness that made her smile. Her eyes twinkled at him and she said,

"I have been lucky to be loved by you!"

"And loved you are, my girl."

They spoke no more about the future. Over time, speech became a greater effort for Grace, so she smiled more and said less. She liked to have Ten Ha sit and chant over her, long droning rhythms that sounded like they came from a gorgeous cave somewhere deep inside him.

Summer coasted to its humid end, nights came a little crisper. Grace pointed out to Marina it was time for her to go back to college.

"No," answered Marina. "It's time for me to be with you."

Grace whispered in raspy protest, struggling for breath and words, "You've got to go. You're my hopes and dreams. Promise me you'll finish college."

"Oh I will." said Marina. "There will be plenty of time. I'll finish school, I'll marry Chance, I'll do all those things."

"I wish you wouldn't!" Grace forced the words out.

"I wouldn't what?"

"Marry Chance." Grace answered, as her head fell back on her pillow, her eyes looked huge as she stared up at Marina.

"Why wouldn't I marry Chance?" Marina asked, wondering if Grace was feverish and not thinking clearly.

"He will hurt you." whispered Grace. "He won't mean to, but he will hurt you."

"Now, now," said Marina. "I know you don't mean that. You rest and I'll come back in a little while with a cup of tea."

"NO!" whispered Grace vehemently, struggling to sit up. "Listen to me!" She gurgled as she spoke, and began to cough. Wet deep wracking coughs. Buddy came in from the kitchen, alarmed.

Grace waved a hand at him and croaked hoarsely, "Go."

He nodded and turned, leaving the room. Marina blinked back tears and her voice shook as she spoke, "I know you love Chance like he is your own. How can you say this? It doesn't make any sense. I love him with all my heart." A tear slid down as she held back a gasp and a sob.

"I know you do." said Grace "but Chance learned lessons early that no child ought to learn. It makes him blind at the times when his heart needs most to see."

Marina's tears dropped silently. "Mimi, you're breaking my heart."

"Oh child, let it break a little now by letting him go, instead of having it smashed to pieces later on. You save your sweet self. Don't marry him, please."

"Don't ask this of me." said Marina. "I love him, I've always loved him. He completes me. I will not give him up!"

Grace lay back, raised her hands and let them drop on her frail birdlike breastbone, exhausted with the effort of trying to move Marina's heart.

Marina whispered to her, "Mimi, I know how much you love me."

Grace nodded at her.

"And I know how wise you are. I know if I could make my head rule my heart, I would do as you ask."

Grace closed her eyes and nodded again.

"But, I cannot. My heart is stronger. I'm sorry."

Grace nodded a third time. She opened her eyes and smiled sweetly at Marina, "You've always had a loving heart; it's been the joy of my life. May it carry you across a sea of sorrow and put you safely on the other side."

Then she closed her eyes again and drifted off to sleep as twilight crept in from the garden. Marina sat and watched her peaceful dreaming, her own thoughts a chaos of confusion and sadness.

Winter came on and Grace died inch by inch, drowning in her failing heart. Marina called Chance in

Italy, telling him it was time to come home and say goodbye.

"I can't." said Chance. "I can't come now. We are in the middle of filming, I can't leave.

"Of course you can." said Marina. "Grace is dying, she needs you here."

"I'm sorry honey, I can't come."

"This is unbelievable! It's a movie, for God's sake. You can put it on hold and finish it later."

"No, I can't." answered Chance. "It's not that simple. A lot of other people are involved, it's a pretty big production. I have to be here and keep it going,"

Marina hung up the phone without another word.

Softly, Grace fell from the living. Gently she opened the fingers of this life and let it ease from her grasp. She pulled each breath unwillingly through the hopeless incoming tide in her lungs. Buddy, Marina, Ten Ha and Tara were gathered round her as she traded water for air one last time. One last exhalation. Then stillness.

For Grace the stillness instantly became floating. She floated slowly up, the ceiling dissolved around her. She found herself looking down on her bed-her own body lay still and a little rumpled, like a cast-off suit of clothes. Buddy was still holding her vacant hand. His upper body stretched across the bed, shoulders heaving in great sobs. Marina, sitting on the other side, was gently stroking the cooling cheek of the body. Ten Ha solemnly intoned sweet prayers to help her on her way. She wished she could drift down and comfort Buddy-tell him everything was alright; but she sensed she could not reach him. That seemed alright as well. She floated up slowly at first and became aware of a great light above her, beckoning; and she flew towards it at ever increasing speed-all thought and feeling falling away from her except the joy of joining with that bright light. She began to move so fast, she seemed to be pulled into and surrounded by a tunnel of light, flying faster and faster toward the source. As she reached the source, there was an ecstatic explosion in her and all around her-cosmically orgasmic beyond all comprehension. Instantly all was soft and perfect darkness. Time and thought and feeling ceased to exist. She just was. She was in loving darkness-nothing else. And nothing else was needed. She was complete.

  Gradually she became aware of velvetiness and then liquid. She was floating in some liquid that was of her and with her and all around her. Next came a sense of gentle vibration. She had no words in her, only feeling. She felt a distant thumping-soft and soothing-always present; a pulsing through the liquid around her and the liquid in her.

  Now came swaying, gurgling. Finally she felt herself: physical. Sonar sounds came through her sweet dark world. She lay dreaming and remembering. Glad for the life of air she once had, and glad for the liquid world of now. She had no sense of time. She became aware of different parts of her body as they slowly appeared. She wiggled some, turned a little, flopping around, loving the water she floated in; curled and harmonious.

  And then, abruptly, her world of water disappeared in a rush. She flailed frantically, terrified to find a raw unsupported world of not-water. She was pulled and pushed down toward the growing light. Sometimes she struggled towards it, feeling unfamiliar friction holding her back. Sometimes she rested, struggling for non-existent air, in lungs unused until this sudden disastrous event.

  All the time, a convulsing movement was contracting and easing, pushing her toward the dim light. And suddenly, she popped out into immense illumination.

Cold cold air rushed into her lungs. A large pink tongue was licking her soft, wet, thick white fur, and as she looked up for the first time into the velvet dark eyes of her mother, all other memories disappeared beneath the surface of her soul, and she was only the child of her mother.

    She was on a rocky beach, wave crash and sucking rolling pebbles were her first sounds. Her mother guided her to her breast. Other seals rolled and snorfled nearby on a cloudy fall day on a Northern California beach.

In the world that Grace left behind, those who loved her tried to pick up the pieces of life without her. Marina and Ten Ha wanted to stay awhile with Buddy to help him through the harsh shards of grief, until time had rounded and melted the cruelest edges. He preferred to be alone. He did not want witness to his sorrow; and he did not want to share the already evaporating spirit of Grace in her house of memories. He didn't want distraction or dilution of any shred of her that he could cling to. Against his strong will, they could only recede and leave him alone.

Ten Ha went back to the temple and resumed the reins as abbot-monk. Marina moved forward with school, mechanically pacing through the work and requirements. She felt drained, devoid of joy. The spring did not beckon to her, and she was indifferent to Chance's absence and to his return. She told him she was numb, grey and raining inside.

In Venice, when Chance heard that Grace was dead, he felt a wall crumple and disintegrate inside. Great waves of hopeless remorse knocked him to the ground and pinned him there. Shep and Sylvia tried to console him.

"I should have gone." said Chance. "How could I have been so stupid! She needed me. I needed to say good-bye. I needed to see her one more time. Marina went through this without me. How could I have been so blind? I left them alone. Why wasn't I there?" He was dumbfounded with surprise at the magnitude of his error. "How could any mistake be this big?" he asked himself. He felt blindsided by something mysterious and unfair. Both Shep and Sylvia had tried to convince him to shelve the movie and go to Grace as she lay dying, but he could not hear the wisdom in their kind attempts to save him from his own poor decision. Now he seemed lost to them, across a gulf made of pain, shame and sorrow.

Ironically, he found himself unable to continue with the film. "Now I've lost the stupid thing I chose, instead of going to Grace."

"It's okay." said Shep. "We've got most of it. I can finish up the filming and wrap things up here. Go home. Go to Marina and Buddy. Talk with Ten Ha. This movie can be put together later, when you're back on your feet."

"I'm letting everybody down." answered Chance, shaking his head and looking down at his hands. "How could I be so stupid, so blind to those I love? I'll never see her again." His voice broke.

Shep patted him clumsily on the shoulder and said, "I'm sorry, man. I wish there was something I could do."

"You did do. You tried to warn me. You tried to get me to do the right thing. I just couldn't see it in time."

"Go on home. Let them help you through it."

"I don't deserve any help. I sure haven't been any help to them. I left Marina to go through it alone."

"She wasn't alone. She had Buddy and Ten Ha."

"Great! She's damn lucky she didn't have to rely on me."

Sylvia had been sitting quietly. Now she spoke in an exasperated tone, "You're a genius, but you're an idiot. Go home!"

A brief grin showed on Chance's face, the first in days. He said, "Thanks Sylvia. Sometimes a little gravel is worth more than a driveway full of syrup. I'll finish up a few loose ends and then get on home, if Shep means it: that he can finish up here. I'm sorry to leave you in the lurch, but I think you're right. I really do need to go home."


When Chance returned to Florida, he and Marina moved into a little cottage on the edge of town, not far from the campus. He blanketed her with sweetness; and the river of time slowly ate at the edges of her grief, until at last the ashy grey fog began to lift and she came back into the world. Even in her pit of loss, she consoled Chance, thinking that guilt was probably a more potent pain than grief, and she knew that Chance was filled with both.

They grew increasingly concerned about Buddy, who seemed to be drifting away. In July, they went to check on him. They drove up to a yard of overgrown grass and a tangle of weeds. Some of Grace's flowers, the dahlias, lilies, and morning glory, accepted the decline in their neighborhood and bloomed on, but the more delicate varieties had been swallowed by nature. The porch had an abandoned look, leaf-litter had gathered in the corners, and a large cobweb stretched across the front door.

They knocked and rang the bell, but heard no sound from within. They walked around to the back and Tara bounded off the porch, black tongue lolling, and fur matted like a winter sheep's. She looked disreputable. The back stoop had several lidless trash cans over-flowing with beer cans, TV dinner wrappings, and more than a few bourbon bottles. Through a grimy window in the backdoor, they could see Buddy with cheeks unshaved, hand wrapped around a beer can, staring into the distance. Chance rapped sharply on the door.

"Buddy, it's us, Chance and Marina."

Buddy sat bolt upright, his eyes became alert as Chance and Marina came through the door. Tara bounded in with them and enthusiastically licked his hand as he stood up. He patted the dog's head absent-mindedly as he looked in wonderment at his visitors.

"Are you really here?" he asked a little suspiciously.

"Yes Buddy, we're really here." said Marina as she moved forward and he engulfed her in a hug.

"Hoo Boy, you stink!" she hooted, but she continued to cling to him, happy just to be with him in his arms. He let go of her and hugged Chance, saying, "What a sight for sore eyes. Why didn't you tell me you were coming? I would have cleaned up a little."

"A little wouldn't have made much difference." observed Marina. "Anyhow, we tried to call; you're not answering your phone."

"Oh yeah, I forgot. I unplugged it because of all those women calling after Grace died. They all wanted to bring round a casserole and console me. I kind of got the feeling a number of them wanted to be interviewed because they thought maybe a vacancy had opened up. Made me mad. Don't get me wrong, a lot of folks were really kind when she died, meant well. But I just don't want to be around them right now.

I guess I forgot and never plugged the phone in again. Well you're here now and that's the main thing. It's mighty nice of you to come see old Buddy and Tara. Care for a beer Chance, or something stronger?"

"No thanks." said Chance. "Looks like you've had enough for both of us!"

"That could be true," replied Buddy, "But how can you tell?"

Marina and Chance both burst out laughing. "Well, the back stoop might have been a little clue!" answered Marina.

Buddy looked out at the trash and said, "I guess I've kind of let things go since Grace died."

"I guess so." responded Marina.

"I can't seem to get a grip on anything." Buddy sounded wistfully perplexed. Then he brightened with an effort. "Well anyhow, how are you two getting along? How's school going, honeybunch?"

"It's going fine, everything is going fine for us, but it looks like things have been going to hell around here."

Buddy's eyes dimmed and he said, "Don't you miss her at all? Don't you care that she's gone?"

"Of course I miss her." said Marina. "I don't do much else, but I'm getting on with it, because that's what she wanted. How do you think she would feel if she could see you like this?"

Buddy pulled himself up tall and said, "I don't guess she'd like it much, but she's not here, is she!"

"No, she's gone and it's just the three of us, and we've got to pull together."

"I don't have much pull left in me." replied Buddy. "I think 'drift' is more my style these days."

"Well Buddy, why don't you drift on down to Florida?" asked Chance. "Ten Ha would like to see you, and that dog of yours looks like she needs a little holiday, she's looking mighty seedy."

Buddy looked down at Tara, aware for the first time of her ragged appearance. "I'm sorry. I guess I didn't realize how dirty she's gotten."

"At least you've been feeding her; she's as round as a barrel." Marina added. "She's not the only one around here who needs a clean-up. Why don't you go take a shower, and get ready to leave with us in the morning."

"I can't leave here!" exclaimed Buddy. "This is where Grace and I lived."

"You need to come be with the living for a while. You know Grace didn't linger here, it's not her style. She wasn't the kind to be a ghost and bother people."

"You got that right!" Buddy flashed back. "She's flat gone! The minute the breath left her body- that was it:

she was gone. I call her name; I try and I try to reach her, but I never get any answer at all. I can't believe there is not one wisp of her left." He looked around at them in agony and confusion, searching their faces for an answer. Then he turned away and stared into the distance, as he had been doing when they arrived. He got up and got a bottle of bourbon from a shelf.

Chance said, "I do know for sure she is not going to be found in the bottom of a whiskey bottle, so maybe you can stop looking for her there."

Buddy looked at him, rubbing his chin. "You don't know much. You didn't even know enough to come home to her when she was dying."

Chance sank into a kitchen chair and said, "I guess maybe there is some truth in that bottle of yours. I'm sorry, Buddy. I'll be sorry all my life. I loved Grace more than any words are ever going tell. And I wish I'd had the sense to be here for her, and for you."

"Pology accepted." said Buddy gravely. "Let's have no more said on the subject." He clapped a hand on Chance's shoulder as Chance sat at Grace's kitchen table. Tears rolled down Chance's face. He wiped away the tears and stood up again,

"Let's get this place cleaned up."

"You go right ahead." said Buddy. "I don't care to be involved myself, but if makes you happy, knock yourselves out."

He sipped his beer and watched the two of them as they spent the evening trying to bring some order to the house Grace had left behind. They ate frozen dinners that Marina found in the freezer, then convinced Buddy to go clean himself up. They all turned in, tired and sad.

They stayed two days, trying to convince Buddy to come back to Florida with them. He refused.

Marina pleaded, "We can't leave you here like this. You can't just let yourself go. Buddy, you've always been a strong man, the strongest I know. Please, please, come with us."

"Sorry Darlin'," he said as he had another sip of whiskey. "I'm not complaining, mind you, but I've gotta say, in my life I've been dealt more than one harsh hand. I've always stood up and I've always gone forward. And then one day, there stood Grace. After that, life held every reward. Our life together was as full as any man could want. She's gone now, life is nothing but emptiness. There's no sense in carrying the load any further. I'm done". He hoisted his glass at them.

Marina was weeping hard. "We need you! You've got to be there for us." Chance's face was bent with pain as he looked at Buddy.

Buddy answered her, "No, you're launched-you're flying high. I'm so proud of you. Proud of you both." He added. "You've got your young life ahead of you. I don't have anything left that I can give you or tell you."

"Please." said Chance- deep solemn need was buried hard in that one word.

"No son. One day you'll understand. Now, say good-bye and take that woman out of here and dry her tears!"

He stood up and gently pushed them toward the screen door. He held the door open and Marina clung to him, crying and crying. Chance stood on the porch searching Buddy's face, as Buddy gently unwrapped Marina's fingers from his shirt front. He kissed her knuckles, patted her closed fist and said,

"See you on down the road."


He died six months later. The whiskey couldn't fill his empty heart or wash away the sadness. Buddy's neighbors said he drowned in whiskey, but Chance knew it was a river of sorrow that pulled him down.

Buddy found himself floating slowly toward the ceiling of the kitchen. As he looked down, he was puzzled by the sight of a man sitting in HIS chair, head and upper body lying across the table. The man's position looked awkward. Buddy felt very peaceful hovering at ceiling level, looking down at the man lying there. Gradually he recognized his own body. He didn't seem to need it any longer.

He drifted up through the rafters, and the attic, and easily through the roofing to a dull cloudy day outside. In spite of the clouds, there was a light glowing above the western horizon. It was different from sunlight, whiter, cooler, but not cold. As he moved through the air toward it, the light began to draw him to itself. He swam gladly into its rays, wanting to reach the source. He went faster and faster, until all was streaking light-brighter and brighter.

Just when he felt himself embraced by the very core of the light, suddenly he popped into utter darkness. It was velvety, and he felt still, calm, peaceful. He had no sense of time. Or of waiting. He just was. Contentedly. A thought dawned slowly-there seemed to be more of him. He was aware of a gentle rhythmic thumping. He felt safe. Surrounded. The gentle rhythm vibrated through him and the liquid in which he floated.

He thought about Grace, Marina, Chance. He remembered the dogs, horses and other animals with whom he'd shared his life. He remembered his mother and father, all of his family and he felt quiet happiness instead of pain in the remembering.

Over some unmeasured span of time he grew bones, a spine. He flexed and kicked and wiggled the miraculous little body he was growing. And then one day he was suddenly pushed, squeezed, convulsed, hurried toward a dim light below him. He swam downward with a feeling of desperation, trying to draw air into his new and unused lungs. He burst out, blinking dimly at a grey sky above, aware mostly of the burning air filling his lungs. Then the sweet caress of his mother's nose. His mind emptied of everything in the past, as he heard the barks and snorts of the seal colony around him.

Within hours, he left the stony beach, and entered into the beckoning and welcoming water. His mother supported him as he tumbled in the shallows, beating his tiny flippers and crying softly to his mother in bleats to say the wonderment was almost more than a little seal could contain. Another little seal, barely one year old, swam to his side and playfully nudged him. He turned round and looked at her with liquid eyes, astonished. She laughed-warm and low. Their Souls were together again-memories were not needed.

Chance and Marina leaned on each other, finding comfort in their shared memories. Marina continued to plod through her final semester of classes, sad and uninspired. Sometimes Chance wondered where she got the strength to go forward, when her heart was so obviously not in her work.

"I just keep remembering how much it meant to Grace and Buddy. I would be betraying them, all the energy and effort they put into helping me get this far. I'm borrowing energy from my own future, I guess. It doesn't feel very good, but I keep telling myself it must be worth it. It just doesn't seem like it now. Surely the sun is going to shine again on me." Then she added plaintively, "Isn't it?"

"Sure, Baby, sure it will!" Chance wasn't so certain, actually. He himself felt wrung out of hope; but he tried to answer her in the way he imagined Buddy might. "This mood is going to pass, Sugar, but it takes some time. Maybe a little visit with Ten Ha? What do you think?"

She shrugged, then agreed. At the temple they found Ten Ha in the sanctuary. Boon-Ho, grinning happily, brought them tea. Ten Ha waited cross-legged on his woven mat while Boon Ho brought sitting-cushions for the guests.

Ten Ha said, "How are my young friends?"

Marina jumped right in, "We're really sad. And I'm pretty angry with Buddy. He didn't care enough about us to even try to take care of himself. He just left us!"

"Don't be angry." said Ten Ha calmly. He gazed serenely into her eyes. "Anger is not good for your mind- try to let anger go. Buddy gave to you, he did not take away. Remember that. It was his time to go. Be grateful to him, because he gave you and Grace so much of himself for a long time."

Marina sat crying, Chance sat silent and wistful.

"Crying is very good." said Ten Ha gently. Your heart is too full of sadness."

"No Ten Ha, it's too empty. It seems like there is nothing left in my heart."

"Just seems that way." answered Ten Ha. "Really, heart too full. It must become more empty to make room for happiness."

"Are you happy?" she asked.

"Happy and sad. Sad not to be with my friends, Grace and Buddy anymore, but also happy."

"Happy how?" asked Chance curiously, leaning forward hoping for something like a lifeline out of his place of grief and despair.

"Can't say." answered Ten Ha. "Not about words, about empty mind. " He smiled sweetly at Chance, who sat upright again with a sad sigh. Marina had stopped crying and was listening.

"Will I EVER understand what you mean?"

"You already understand, just don't know it." he said placidly. He changed the subject abruptly, "How is field study now?"

"I've pretty much lost interest." she answered. "You know, first I was with Grace, then after she died I didn't really care about the study and now with Buddy gone…" she trailed off, hunching her shoulders.

"I think you may want to do study some more now. Birds are here now from the north. It is right time to do good work. You are helping scientific understanding."

"I know I should." Marina said unhappily. "I just can't seem to make myself start again. I'm just too ... sad. It's as much as I can do to get through my class work."

"Go do field study for yourself. If you will be out in nature, your heart will begin to be more empty of sadness."

"Chance has been pushing me to get back into it. They could really use another person out there."

"Yes," said Chance, "Why don't you go talk to Professor Tamlin tomorrow. I'm sure he'll be thrilled. Well, he won't act thrilled- I know he hasn't been very understanding about what you're going through, but he will be thrilled to have you back."

She asked Chance, "What will you do, if I'm in the field. I don't want to go off and leave you alone, all sad and everything."

"No problem." said Ten Ha. "Maybe Chance can take me to the river. We can visit with the birds who have come for the winter. I have never been on this river."

"That's a great idea!" said Chance. "We can do a canoe trip for a week along the river." He turned to Marina, "Will you be alright with that?"

"Of course I will. I think you should go."

Chance started planning immediately, "I'll call Mark, he's been wanting to come down from Connecticut. He can handle the front of the canoe. But, " he tapped Ten Ha's knee, "we'll need to go soon. Shep and Sylvia will be home soon, and Shep and I need to get started on the film."

"Soon is good," responded Ten Ha. "But, I do not know how to work a canoe."

Chance told him he could sit in the middle and would not have to paddle.

"Good. I am very skilled at sitting."

They left the temple feeling better. Ten Ha had been a part of Grace's and Buddy's life. Being with him seemed to bring back some little pieces of them. Also, Ten Ha was older-that was comforting to them both. His light handed guidance made them feel less alone. That night they slept in each other's arms more lightly and tranquilly.

The next day, Professor Tamlin was indeed gruff and gave Marina a stern lecture on professional responsibility, and the need to place work above emotion. She thought to herself that he was a troll in shallow boots, but she held her tongue, 'yes-sired', and was back in the swamp that afternoon after classes.

She took a desultory interest in the patch of nature about which she had previously been so passionate. A few nuthatches were busy near the stand where she sat, a deer came by nibbling casually, and several young squirrels romped right over her foot. She mechanically recorded each presence. The day was pleasantly cool, the sky was blue, and the sun slanted under the tree branches, brightening spots on the ground and illuminating the white plumage of an egret resting on a low branch. She didn't realize she was breathing deeply, relaxed, more peacefully. The world still showed nothing but dulled colors to her, but a gentle easing had begun.

Shortly before sunset a hush fell across the swamp where she sat. She looked around, perplexed by the sudden silence. Normally the birds had a lot to say as they finished their activities for the day and sought their roosts. She could see the egret on the branch looking intently at something in the river. Something large and white was moving through the shallows. Slowly a white alligator walked out of the water onto the muddy flat bank.

As Marina watched mesmerized, the largest alligator she had ever imagined emerged and walked steadily toward the platform. It was dull white, slightly beige in some of its markings. As it approached she could see it had golden eyes. Its iris' were so metallic she wondered if it was blind. There was no sound except her breathing and a swashing sound as its belly and tail scraped through the grass.

When it reached the base of the platform, it eased down onto its stomach, settled in and sighed. Marina, looking directly down, saw what looked like an enormous ruby set in the middle of the animal's forehead. She guessed the creature was at least eighteen feet long. It opened its jaws and lay with its mouth gaping. Marina was transfixed. It looked like a carved graven image come to life. As she peered down she decided it must be blind, then it rolled its golden eyes up at her, pupils opening, and it looked steadily at her.

Marina felt her mind expanding oddly-it was calming to look into those great metallic eyes. She felt the immense power of the animal's thoughts, deep but uncomplicated-older than any thoughts the primate part of her brain had bequeathed to her. Then, the alligator closed its eyes, closed its mouth and appeared to go to sleep. The birds began to sing again as if they had never been silent. The frogs who had been quiet began to chorus and splash.

She waited as long as she dared, hoping the alligator would depart; but at last as the sun was sinking she made her way down the ladder and tiptoed past the Andeluvian giant. It opened one eye. Her heart almost stopped. It closed its eye again and smiled faintly as she walked away as stealthily as she could. When she got around the first bend in the path she ran as fast as she could to her car, putting distance between her and the beast. She was also trying to beat the darkness that was creeping through the woods.

When she got home, she told Chance about the encounter.

"Oh God, let's get some lights and the camera. We've got to film it!"

"No Chance, I don't want to."

"Are you scared, Baby? I can go by myself."

"No, it's not that I'm scared, although I was when I had to walk past it. It's just that it felt, I don't know, sacred or something. I don't think I want to dilute my sense of the mystical power. It felt like the Alligator God chose to come and spend a little time with me, a blessing or a gift. I don't know, but I don't want to cheapen or profane or normalize anything about this experience."

"What are you going to say in the field notes?" asked Chance.

"Nothing."

"You're not going to write it up?"

"No, I'm going to let it be."

"That's not very scientific of you."

"No, but it's respectful. If anybody even believed me, there would be a team out tomorrow stalking the animal, trying to catch it. They would torture it with tests then dissect it to accumulate a data base. I've noticed a curious lack of comprehension in some of the departments. Several otherwise very bright people haven't yet noticed that if they disassemble an animal, no matter how carefully they re-assemble the parts, something vital is missing!"

"Point taken." answered Chance dryly.


Very early the next morning while Marina was in class, Chance drove out to the research stand. He approached, camera in hand, and found the student on duty was snoozing in her chair, hat pulled down over her eyes. Chance quietly examined the ground in front of the stand, finding the grass and wet earth impressed and flattened where the giant white alligator had lain. The grass was smashed down and muddied where it had walked back to the riverbank in the dark. The size of its footprints in the mud was startling.

Chance filmed the prints, and then walked back to the stand, filming the path of the reptile. As he zoomed in on the ground where the alligator had clearly lain, he saw flashes of gold through his lens. He knelt to the ground and still filming, put out his hand and picked up three small golden objects-two seals and a dolphin. They looked like charms from a bracelet. He silently put them in his pocket, and strolled back through the woods to his truck.

At dinner, Marina talked more about the encounter with the alligator. Chance didn't mention that he had been out to the site.

That night he dreamed he was in the stand with Marina, and the white alligator was lying beneath, on the ground looking up at them. Marina climbed down the ladder and walked carefully past the beast. When Chance climbed down, the alligator swung his head savagely and snapped, driving Chance back up the ladder. Marina looked back from the edge of the forest and called to him. She hadn't seen the alligator turn on him.

"Just walk quietly past him. Just think calm and sweet thoughts, he won't hurt you."

"I can't get past him. He won't let me by." he called back to her in the dream. The alligator snapped his jagged teeth, watching Chance intently.

Finally Chance reached into his pocket and threw down the three golden trinkets. The alligator delicately picked up each one, using his enormous tongue. He then walked deliberately to Marina who was still waiting on the path at the edge of the dark woods. Chance leapt to the ground and ran in a slow motion dream pace, unable to reach her in time to protect her. As he watched horrified and helpless, the giant animal opened its mouth as wide as it could, the golden trinkets glistening on its tongue. Marina reached down into the creature's mouth and retrieved the little animal charms. When her hand had left its mouth, the alligator slowly closed its jaw. Marina reached out a tentative hand then laid her palm gently on the white bony snout. The alligator closed its eyes. After a few seconds it turned slowly and gracefully, then walked back to the water. As it passed Chance, Chance could see his own face reflecting in the red jewel on the alligator's forehead. The beast snapped at him but kept walking.

Chance woke up shouting. Marina switched on the bedside light and leaned over him. "You were having a bad dream. It's alright," she said, "it was just a dream."

Chance struggled from under the bed covers and retrieved his pants from where he had thrown them on the floor when he went to bed. He reached in the pocket, then wordlessly handed the three trinkets to her. She put on her reading glasses and after examining them exclaimed, "They're gorgeous! What a beautiful gift. Where on earth did you get them? I've never seen anything like them."

"Never mind," he answered. "They're for you." He climbed back into bed and fell into profound sleep. She continued to sit and examine, fascinated by the beautiful tokens of his love. Finally she turned off the light and drowsed off curled up against his warm back, touched by the strange and wondrous gift.

In the morning she thanked him again. He smiled a little sheepishly and said, "Don't mention it."

She thought she would spend her lunch break shopping for a bracelet to hold the charms. Chance quickly said,

"Oh let me get it for you. Or better yet, how about a necklace. That way you can wear them all the time. A bracelet will be a nuisance for you."

"You've already given me these incredible charms. I can get the necklace."

"No, no, I insist." he said. "I want to!"

"Okay." she smiled. "You are really sweet. You're really spoiling me. And I like it."

"I should spoil you more than I do." he said, looking down at his coffee.

She came over behind where he was sitting and hugged his shoulders. "What were you dreaming about last night? You were running in place like Bayou used to, when he was dreaming."

"I was dreaming about your big white alligator. He wasn't very keen on me in the dream. "

Marina swung her head down and around and looked at his face, as she continued to hug him around the back of his seat. "What do you think it means?"

He pulled her around toward her and kissed her. "I think he was telling me not to mess with your magic."

She patted him on the head, then gathered her books and papers and did dancing leaps to the door, where she turned and blew him a kiss and left for the day. He finished his coffee, sat thoughtfully for a few more minutes then drove downtown to a jewelry store.

When Marina came home, he laid a blue velvet jewelry case on the table in front of her. She opened it breathlessly. Inside was a gold chain, each link shaped like a heart. A little gold dog hung from the chain."

"It's Bayou!"', she said.

"Yep," said Chance. "He was our first link. You only took me home because of Bayou."

"Yeah," she said laughing, "I had to take the boy if I wanted the dog, it was a package deal."

She got out the little gold seals and dolphin. Chance attached them to the chain using a pair of needle-nosed pliers. He fastened the necklace around her neck and she fingered the charms.

"I've never cared a bit about jewelry," she said, "But this means so much. What made you decide on seals and a dolphin?"

"Actually I didn't choose them. A friend of yours did."

"What friend?" she asked, puzzled.

"The big white alligator."

"What!" She stared at him.

He told her about his visit to the stand. She was speechless.

Finally she said, "That's very strange." She fingered the charms again and re-examined them. "They are incredible. I don't know what to think of them." She looked at him sharply. "I can't believe you went there to try and film him after I said I didn't want you to!"

"I'm sorry, Sweetie. I just couldn't let an opportunity like that go by. It was a once in a lifetime encounter. It ought to be documented."

"Chance, there's a lot that ought not to be documented. Sometimes there are mysteries that are too powerful and deeply meaningful. They should not be defined, measured, recorded, or even talked about in an idle way."

"Why? Do they lose their power, their magic?" he asked her.

"No, but we can lose our ability to be open to the power and magic if we disrespect the sacred mysteries we are fortunate enough to be permitted to share."

"I can't see it." responded Chance, frustrated again by the feeling that those who were important to him always seemed to grasp something that was invisible to him.

"I know." Marina's voice was tender, a little regretful as well.

"But you love me anyway." he said bitterly.

"I love you." was her reply.

When Chance suggested the canoe trip to him, Mark rearranged his calendar and was ready to start in a week. Before he left Manhattan, he visited a venerable and ancient shop that outfitted fly fisherman, explorers, and even wealthy adventurers. The store had been in existence for over a hundred years. Mark emerged from the place empty handed, the merchant having suggested they ship his purchases directly to Orange Blossom.

He arrived at Chance's house, eager to get on the river. He asked if his equipment had arrived yet. Chance opened the door to the spare room and gestured, saying, "We're not towing a barge behind the canoe, you know!"

The room was stuffed full of esoteric and expensive outdoor equipment. Mark peered in through the door. "I thought I might be overdoing it a little. It all seemed like a good idea at the store."

"You can probably leave the navigational instruments, short wave radio and the hip waders. Bug-hat might come in handy though."

When Chance finished the triage, Mark had a very small pile of clothes, four cans of elegant smoked sausages, and two bottles of red wine..

"Are you sure?" he asked Chance as he looked wistfully at the heap of expensive and useless gadgets. "What about the hand-carved Algonquin paddle?"

"Sure, take it too." said Chance generously. "It's a bit long in the handle and wide in the blade-it would tire me out in a hurry."

"I think I'll take it." said Mark, happily. He poked through the pile and extracted three cases of fishing poles. "Don't you think these could be handy?"

"Not with Ten Ha along. He won't say anything, but I know he would rather we didn't kill anything."

"Oh yes, of course." Mark regretfully put back the poles.

The next morning, they picked up Ten Ha and drove out to Orange Blossom. The big old aluminum canoe was behind the travel trailer, where Chance had left it months ago. It was Mark's turn to laugh when he saw it.

"That's our mighty vessel? I was picturing Kevlar, or at least a wooden Old Towne."

"See the dents?' asked Chance.

"Yes."

"Alligator snouts." he said solemnly.

"Really?" asked Mark.

"No," laughed Chance, "but there are a lot of snags and cypress knees hidden just below the surface. You really need an old beater boat to take all the banging around. "

"It looks big enough, at least." observed Mark.

"It shrinks when you put all the gear in!"

Mark and Ten Ha carried it to the water's edge and set it down in the water, with its bow pulled up onto the sandy bank. It took a couple of hours to pack everything in; a week's worth of food for three men took up a lot of room. When the canoe was loaded it was so heavy it took all the strength they had to pull it off the bank. And when they were all aboard, the boat was riding very low in the water.

They paddled downstream through tea-coloured translucent water. The boat only showed about three inches of freeboard and Mark warned Ten Ha not to lean outboard,

"We'll be looking at the surface from the bottom side."

"No problem." responded Ten Ha. "Balance is good practice for monk. Especially because I see some eyes of alligator friends looking at me very mindfully. They are excellent influence to remind monk to stay balanced."

The current was of medium swiftness, and the three friends relaxed and enjoyed the passing scenery in the jungle swamp. They were slathered in herbal oils, so the mosquitoes and gnats left them alone. Mark occasionally pointed with his paddle blade, indicating to Chance there was an underwater snag to avoid; and Chance leisurely guided them around the bends of the river deeper into the cypress world.

Among the many birds, they saw large herons-white and blue, snowy egrets, gallinules, and moorhens. Birds were everywhere, and turtles on every log-sometimes lined up, sometimes just hanging quietly in the water. Alligators from small to large were sunning in the shallows, laying among the weeds. Twice they spotted small deer standing back from the shore in the swamp forest, alert-eyed with muzzles up.

The men glided silently along, enfolded in the hot sleepy moist and secret world. The abundance of life, the generosity of nature in that place filled them completely with the goodness of the day, and left no room for any sad or bitter thoughts.

The mullet rose continually to the surface, sucking air greedily through lush thick fish lips. Hyacinths and water lilies floated their buds and flowers above and below the surface of the water. Bright sleek frogs rode the lily pads unfazed by the passing canoe. Silently, each man drifted in his own mind as the miles floated by.

In the late afternoon they spotted a good sized hummock of dry land and decided to camp for the night. They tied the canoe alongside a fallen tree and walked along its wide old trunk to reach the earth. Ten Ha gathered firewood and dry Spanish moss for fire-start. Mark carried the gear and food, while Chance put up the tent.

"We'll have to take turns tonight, keeping the fire built up and watching for gators." Chance informed them.

"And what do we do if we see a gator?" asked Mark trying to sound unconcerned.

"Wave a fiery torch at it, it will go away."

They built a smoky fire by mixing green wood with dry. The smoke drove the flying insects away and as darkness fell the birds found their nightly roosts and settled down, while the woods came awake with noises and motions that Mark had never heard before.

Ten Ha said happily, "Sounds like jungle I visited with my father, when very young boy." Mark sat on a fallen log. He put his hands behind his head and sighed contently,

"It's really good to be outdoors! My thoughts were getting pretty stale."

"You can feed your stale thoughts to those fish. Maybe fresh thoughts for them." Ten Ha gestured toward the Mullets who were rising, their lips forming lazy circling ripples on the surface. Then he cooked a pot of rice, and they ate whatever was at hand. They talked a little. Ten Ha scraped the left over rice from the pot into the river to feed the fish, while Mark and Chance took a pull or two from a whiskey bottle.

Chance and Ten Ha went to sleep while Mark kept watch for a while. Through the tops of the trees he could see little patches of the night sky. Humidity hid most of the stars but here and there they twinkled, and a planet shone brightly. It felt good to him to be awake and keenly aware, watching for a stealthy large reptile and ready to invoke the rule of fire to drive back that ancient hunter of men. When he played his flashlight over the surface of the darkened river, he would find red eyes glowing back at him but no one approached the camp.

At last his eyes began to droop and he changed places with Chance, who watched through the long hours; enjoying the bonfire and the age old night. Well before dawn Ten Ha took over and guarded them. As the new day was approaching he began his daily chants, greeting the sun and giving thanks. Several alligators nearby were moved to respond with their booming voices as he chanted in the day.

In the morning, the world was wringing wet from a dewfall as heavy as rain. The air was a little cool, and hot coffee and tea felt robust. They fried some eggs and toast, then spent an hour packing up and breaking camp. The heavy canoe wallowed as they boarded. They slipped away down the river looking forward to another steamy day in the jungle.

By midafternoon, all three had reached a dreamy meditative state of mind and so were not alert as they swept around a tight bend and encountered a large fallen tree, crossing the river like a bridge. The bottom of the trunk was only about two and a half feet above the river and before they knew it, the bow of the canoe was already passing under the tree. Mark leaned back as Ten Ha leaned forward. They cracked their heads together, and then both leaned sharply toward the right side of the canoe.

In a split second the boat capsized, and they were all in the water. The overloaded canoe sank abruptly out of sight, while Ten Ha was being quickly dragged under by the weight of his heavy waterlogged robes. Mark handed him the carved Algonquin paddle which gave him enough flotation to keep his head just barely above water. When he saw that the monk was in no danger of immediate drowning, Chance couldn't help laughing, saying he looked a lot like a mullet with just his lips showing above water sometimes.

The banks of the river were lined with big gnarly roots, tangled several feet above the water, with no place to get out. The thought of alligators was in everybody's mind. They kept together, treading water, being swept along by the moderate current. Another downed tree loomed into sight ahead of them, fallen over the water. It was only about eighteen inches above the surface. Chance was hopeful they could somehow hold on to it and pull themselves up.

They were almost to the tree when a large black bear walked out onto the fallen tree, balanced on all fours and looked right at them. They swam in desperation toward the side of the river farthest from the bear but they didn't get far. The bear lay belly down on the tree trunk, reached down and grasped Chance inside his armpits, then flopped him up and over the tree trunk as easily as if he were a wet towel being hung over the line.

Ten Ha grabbed hold of the tree trunk over his head and kicked his legs against the current, not wanting to leave Chance behind. Mark caught hold of a cypress knee just on the other side of the tree. The bear reached his paw down towards Ten Ha's hand and Ten Ha reached out and grasped it.

"God dammit!" yelled Mark. "What the hell are you doing?"

Ten Ha had given the bear his other hand by then and the bear lifted him straight out of the water and placed him on the log. He wound up sitting on the trunk next to the bear.

Mark sputtered, "Get the hell out of there, Ten Ha. That's a bear! A bear! Dangerous! Jump in and swim."

"It's no problem." said Ten Ha. "I think the bear wants to help."

"No, Ten Ha, it's a wild animal. Jump and swim away!"

A large man appeared out of the woods, saying in a thick voice, "It's okay, it's okay, the bear is friendly." The stranger spoke again, "Do you want to come home with me and Ur?"

"Yes." said Ten Ha promptly.

"We ought to go see about raising the canoe." said Chance.

The stranger said, "I'm going home now." He then turned around and disappeared into the woods. The bear remained and followed them as they worked their way over torturous roots, falling into deep mud holes and keeping a watchful eye for alligators. It took them about an hour to go the short distance back to the tree where they had capsized.

Chance jumped into the river and dove beneath the surface. When he came up, the bear offered him a paw and hauled him back up onto the root mat.

"I can't find the bottom, let alone the canoe. I think we've got a problem here."

Mark tried diving into the muddy river and Ten Ha probed around with a long pole. The river had formed a deep hole there, and the canoe was gone.

The bear began to shamble off into the woods but stopped and looked back at them. He went a little further then looked back again. He returned to the men then started off again.

Ten Ha said, "Good idea to go with bear, I think."

They picked their way slowly. The bear stopped frequently and waited for them to catch up. After a long hour of falling, staggering, and balancing on knotty roots, they came to a dwelling. It was an incredible hodge-podge of an old shack, repaired and maintained with cypress logs, old boards and various random-looking materials. The roof was a crazy-thatch of palmetto leaves. The building had long ago traded any semblance of square for a more organic and amorphous shape. It sat on a good sized wharf, also held together with old vines and miscellaneous boards.

There was a ladder fixed to the wharf. Several rungs had been replaced with tree branches broken to the proper length then bound in place with vines. Someone had done a handsome job wrapping the vines. At the end of the wharf farthest from the building was a fire pit built up on a mound of earth surrounded by branches, Lincoln-logged to hold the dirt in place. The strange man from the riverbank was seated in front of the fire watching something cook on a metal rack that looked like it came from an old refrigerator.

There were halves of coconut shells sitting nearby, serving as bowls. He waved his wooden pronged poking stick at them and said, "I'm Johnny and I'm home. Now Ur is home, too." And he shook with happy laughter. "Let's eat."

The bear lay down next to Johnny, sniffing at the meat and fish on the grill.

"We are extra lucky." said Johnny, grinning wide. "Ur brought deer yesterday. We hardly ever have deer." He bounced a little and smiled a bit wider.

Ten Ha said, "I have a friend like you at home. His name is Boon-Ho. I think you and I will be friends."

Johnny beamed at him and said, "Friends. Ur is friends, too."

The bear lifted his head and looked at the three visitors, as if agreeing with Johnny's appraisal of the situation. Johnny repeated each of their names several times as they introduced themselves, then turned back to the fire saying, "Oh! Oh no! Oh, food is in trouble!"

The bear looked at the grill and looked at Johnny, then settled his head on his paws again. Johnny poked and turned and hollered a little and then grunted softly and said, "Okay. It's okay. Food is good!"

He counted on his fingers twice and set out five square pieces of banana leaves on the deck, counting aloud as he placed them.

He took the bits of meat and fish off the grill and carefully placed them on the leaves. He spent some time counting the pieces of food until he was satisfied there was an equal amount on each leaf. He had two pieces remaining, which he added to one of the helpings, explaining,

"For Ur because Ur is bigger. So Ur gets more." He nodded to himself, and then he carefully handed the leaf to Ur who immediately ate everything, leaf included, in one mouthful. Johnny laughed with obvious delight, then he handed round the food to his visitors. It was very tasty. They ate quickly and hungrily, and then wiped their fingers on the leaves, and threw the leaves on the fire.

Mark said to Ten Ha, "I thought you didn't eat meat or fish."

Ten Ha answered, "I prefer no animals are killed, but what is given to me, I eat. And monk is grateful to the giver, does not matter the gift."

Mark asked Johnny how long he had been living in his house. Johnny scratched his head and thought. "I don't know. A long time, I think. I like it here, home is good. " Ur grunted softly."Yes, we like it here." Johnny finished.

"Do you ever go out of the swamp?" asked Chance.

"Just a little." answered Johnny. "Sometimes we go to the picnic place to find things. Sometimes we go to the edge of the trees to get fruit that is growing there. Oranges, bananas, some green fruit, I don't know what it is. But it is good!" he announced with great relish. Ur grunted happily again at the sound of Johnny's pleasure.

"It must be a lot of work to find enough food for you and a pet bear." ventured Mark.

Johnny laughed and rocked softly to and fro. "A lot of trouble for UR! Ur gets the food mostly. But," he said abruptly, "I help," and he pointed his thumb at himself. "Yes, I help."

The day was ending and the men were weary from the afternoon's exertion.

"How far is it to get out of here?" asked Chance.

"Far." answered Johnny, looking sad. "You are not going today. It is too far. It takes one whole day to go to the picnic place, look for good things, then carry them home. This is home!" he announced, turning and extending his arm as if he were lord of a magnificent estate. Ten Ha giggled, so Johnny giggled as well.

"You can stay in our home tonight. It's very hot so Ur will want to sleep outside. Too many bugs so I will sleep inside. When it is cold Ur sleeps inside. He hugs me all night and I am always warm even when it is cold outside." He beamed with satisfaction. Ur got up, walked to Johnny and placed a paw on his knee.

"Ur thinks I need to go to bed. " said Johnny "Ur is smarter than me."

"I don't know about that." said Mark. "I don't know anyone else smart enough to have a bear for a friend."

Johnny laughed hard, his shoulders heaving like jelly. "You are a funny man."

As they were talking, Ur walked to the door of the dwelling. The door was made of deer-hide stretched on willow sticks, and hinged with strips of hide. Ur swung open the door and Johnny rose and walked heavily across the deck. He bent down and went inside. They heard his thick muffled voice,

"You can sleep in my home if you want to."

Chance said to his friends, "I'll go have a look, tell you what I think."

He hunched over and entered. He found a dimly lit, immaculately clean, oddly shaped room. It seemed a combination of an animal's burrow and a fishing camp. There was a battered table with one leg missing and a stick lashed in its place. A motley assortment of utensils lay on the table along with a coconut hull, clean and full of clear water. In a dark corner, away from the door was a sweet smelling bed of dried fern fronds and cattails, covered with a tattered piece of old quilt.

"What a great place to sleep!" exclaimed Chance.

"My bed." said Johnny proudly. "Ur gets plants for me and puts them in the sun to dry, so I can have a good bed."

"Ur takes good care of you, doesn't he?"

"Yes, Ur is my friend. My only friend until you came."

"Don't you have any family?" asked Chance.

"Had family. They were very mean to me because I am not smart. So when I grew up, I came here. I like it here. I like home and I like Ur."

Chance nodded at the sweet and simple man, and then looked around the curious house, charmed by what he found. The decaying window frames had been replaced with curving honeysuckle. Screen had been stretched haphazardly over the vine, and Spanish moss was tucked carefully in every crack and crevice. Some kind of greenery was shredded and strewn on the floor and window ledges.

"What is that?" asked Mark, who had come inside.

"For bugs." Johnny slapped at his arms to demonstrate. "Bugs don't like this plant. Ur brings it, and I," here he pointed at his chest, "I tear them up and walk on them so they smell. Smells good to me, but smells bad to bugs." He smiled triumphantly. "I can take some of my bed and give it to everyone."

"No, no, that's okay. We'll just sleep on the floor," said Mark. "There's not enough bedding there to make three more beds comfortably. No point in making yourself uncomfortable for no reason."

Johnny looked at him in bewilderment. "I don't understand what you said. You don't want me to share?"

Ten Ha overheard the conversation as he came through the door. "No problem." he said soothingly. "We will be more happy on the floor."

"Why?" asked Johnny.

"Because we will be more happy to see you sleeping in one big bed."

"Okay." said Johnny. He lay down on his pile of soft bracken. In less than half a minute he was gently snoring. Ur closed the leather door and they heard him settle against it as he, too, dozed off for the night.

"No fear of gators tonight." observed Mark.

"Yes, I could sleep on a bed of nails." added Ten Ha.

Mark glanced at him quickly.

"Monk joke." said Ten Ha as he also settled easily onto the wooden floor. Curled up against the walls, they all enjoyed deep sleep after an exhausting day.

In the morning Johnny agreed to take them to the picnic place. As they were washing in the creek by the shack, the bear came out of the woods carrying a bucket full of bananas, oranges, a couple of avocados and one perfectly ripe papaya. He poured them out on the deck, retreated a few steps, sat down and swept a paw in the air.

Chance said, "It looks like he is inviting us to breakfast."

"He is." Johnny told him. "Ur brings breakfast every morning."

"Where does he get it?" asked Chance as he dried his hands on the sides of his pants which were still damp from yesterday's dunking.

"Trees." answered Johnny, starting to methodically peel an orange.

"Trees in an orchard?"

"I don't understand what you mean. I don't know what is orchard" Johnny was puzzled, orange juice dripped onto his shirt as he chewed and thought.

"A place with a lot of orange trees all together." suggested Ten Ha".

"No," said Johnny slowly, continuing to think. "Just one orange tree, just one banana tree. They live with all these other trees." He indicated the native species growing all around his house. "But, only more small."

"So Ur doesn't get them where people are growing them?" Mark asked.

"NO! No! NO!" Johnny became excited and upset. "People try to hurt Ur. Ur NEVER goes where people are. Two times a man shot his gun at UR at the picnic place. No! Ur NEVER NOT go where people are!"

Ur had risen and was standing upright in front of Johnny. The bear sniffed the air and peered at the visitors, trying to find the threat. When Johnny became less panicked, the bear dropped to all fours. He sat close to Johnny and watched him. Johnny reached out a hand and clutched the bear's fur.

"I love Ur."

The bear put its great paw over Johnny's hand. Johnny smiled, his agitation fading.

"Why do you call him Ur?', asked Mark

"That's his name."

"How do you know that?"

"Ur told me."

"He told you?"

"Yes, When Ur found me, I said to him, 'My name is Johnny. What is your name?' and he told me 'Ur'."

"Then Ur it is." said Ten Ha. He smiled at man and bear. "I am very happy to meet you both, Johnny and Ur. And I thank you for helping us."

Johnny beamed. "I am happy we are helping. Now, I am going to the picnic place. Come on, Ur."

He got up, climbed down the ladder and walked off into the woods. The men scrambled to catch up. Johnny stopped and told them, "Ur goes first. Only Ur knows how to find the picnic place."

After four long hours of picking their way through the swamp, they were sure only Ur knew the way. They were tired, muddy and bug bitten. Ur and Johnny seemed fresh and spry. Ur stopped and Johnny said, "Ur says 'good-bye'. He stays here so people cannot see him. He waits for me and he will take me home."

Mark and Chance nodded to the bear, but Ten Ha walked over to him and put out his hand, saying, "Good-bye my friend. Thank you."

The bear gently pressed the monk's hand between his two paws and bowed his head, then released Ten Ha's hand. Johnny was already walking toward the thinning of the forest. Within a few minutes they came out into the mowed orderliness of a state park picnic area.

Johnny excitedly rummaged through the nearest trash can and found an almost new tee shirt. "Hee hee, new clothes for Johnny!" he cried in a singsong voice.

The men tried to thank him and say good-by but they could barely pull his attention away from his happy foraging. He waved one hand and said,

"Bye-bye." Then he turned his back to them and continued looking for useful things. They walked out to the nearby road and went a short distance to a gas station. As they walked, Chance asked the other two,

"Do you think we should try to get him some assistance? Can we give him something? Help him out?"

"He needs nothing." observed Ten Ha.

"I agree." seconded Mark. "If we interfere, our good intentions will probably bring nothing but trouble for him and the bear. I don't think anyone else will take such good care of him as that bear is already doing. More likely, some do-gooder will shoot or cage the bear, and probably put Johnny in something very like a cage."

"I guess you're right." said Chance. "Guess I'll have to forego the documentary, huh?"

"I don't know." quipped Mark. "You've already faced an angry Victoria, I think a bear might be less frightening."

Chance paused and didn't laugh at this reminder of his slip in judgment, when he had aired 'A Studied Woman'.

Ten Ha spoke, "Better for Johnny, better for bear if you leave story untold."

"But it's amazing. " Chance wrestled with himself. "And it deserves to be told; it should be filmed."

"Bear and man deserve to be left alone. Maybe real lives more important than story lives."

Chance was startled by what Ten Ha said. "I never thought about it that way. You know my vision, my art, it is who I am. As a being, this is who I am!"

"Maybe," said the monk, "Maybe not."

"What's that mean, oh Cryptic One?"

"Being has three dimensions, is deep. Film just two dimensions-just surface." answered Ten Ha, his face impassive.

Mark glanced over at him, then at Chance to see how Chance would react to that comment. Chance said nothing, but looked puzzled and thoughtful as they walked into the gas station. He called Marina from the pay phone, and then the three men sat silently on a bench in front of the station. The monk was silent by nature, Chance by inner rumination, and Mark because he felt an awkward tension. Gradually they began to chat lightly about the previous day; and the heaviness between them sunk down beneath the surface of their friendship.

By the time Marina pulled up in the truck, they were lighthearted again and joking with each other. Tara bounced out of the back of the pickup and pushed her head against Ten Ha's knee with hard affection. After that, she rubbed her wooly cheek enthusiastically against Chance's thigh. She stopped abruptly and sniffed him hard, whiffling a little in her intensity. She sniffed all over Ten Ha. Then looked around to see what an Ur-odored creature looked like. She had never encountered bear aroma before, but it was obvious to her that she was having a close sniff of a large meat-eating animal. She seemed reassured after peering around and listening, finding no one. She went back to studying the smell closely, creating an idea in her mind of what Ur must be.

While the men had been on the river, most of the movie crew had returned from Venice. James and his wife, Louise, stayed on in Europe; but Sylvia, Shep and Marie were at Miss Margaret's when Marina brought the bedraggled campers home. When the river mud had been scrubbed off, everyone met in the parlor for what became a raucous re-union. They danced, sang, and drank Miss Margaret's bourbon into the wee hours, until Sheriff Ray and his deputy arrived sometime after midnight responding to a call from a neighbor complaining about the racket. The sheriff suggested they tone it down and Shep suggested the sheriff lighten up instead. At about two in the morning, the neighbor who called in the complaint came over to complain in person. He was scandalized to see the sheriff playing a guitar and singing the loudest. The sheriff suggested there was an ordinance about disturbing the fun; but Miss Margaret said she thought it was time to break it up before someone wound up in jail or out of office. The sheriff and deputy drove away singing loudly, turning on the siren as they went past the house of the disgruntled neighbor. The remaining guests filled a few of the musty bedrooms in the old mansion and everyone except Ten Ha and Tara slept until noon.

  Mark and Marie left for Connecticut the next afternoon and Marina and Ten Ha went back to the city. Chance stayed in Orange Blossom. He and Shep were ready to submerge themselves in the editing of 'The Art of Losing.'

Shep said, "I knew I could never film those last few scenes the way you would have, so I didn't even try. I'm hoping we can change the mood of the film at the end when it becomes clear that she really is an angel; that we can use the change in filming style as an aid to relay that idea. So, I tried to get the actors to go deeper, look for richer, more complex aspects of the characters. I think we can weave in some of your beautiful footage of the place to help with continuity, and transition the look of the film."

"Let's see what we've got." suggested Chance.

They skimmed through the footage they had filmed together using a simple editing machine to view it. After that they watched the new footage on good sized screen. When it was over, Chance slapped Shep on the knee, saying, "Great stuff, man! We are going to cook us up one heck of a movie! You've brought so much depth to the characters and the story. I can really see it now, in this new footage."

They settled down to the job and worked at it for a couple of months. By early summer it was ready to premiere. Marie arranged for the first screening to be in Los Angeles, hoping it would catch the eye of someone at one of the big movie companies. It was an immediate hit; all three big companies bid and bargained against each other for the rights. Thanks to Marie's hard-nosed attitude, Spanish Moss Productions came away with full pockets and no undesirable commitments.

James and Louise Mulligan came to town for the premiere. James was wooed by several producers but he smiled and walked away. The Italian version of Hamlet had made him a superstar in France, Germany and Italy. While Shep and Chance had been editing 'The Art of Losing', he and Louise had bought a small farm in the south of France.

"A farm in France! For crying out loud!" Matt Starling, the latest hottest producer in Hollywood was aghast. "Didn't you go into acting to get off the farm? With your face and your talent, not to mention that voice, you don't ever have to work outdoors again! Hollywood is just crying out for a fresh new black star. You're going to be the next Sydney Poitier, for Chrissakes."

"I think Sydney Poitier is doing a pretty good job of being Sydney Poitier. I'll do a movie when I see something that interests me. But you know what I've discovered? I like farming real well when I own the farm! I'm going to take all that movie money and plow it into that good, rich, well-draining Provence soil, and grow some lavender and some olive trees."

"Lavender and olives." muttered Starling as he walked away. "Of all the crazy ideas…"

The Mulligans went home to Orange Blossom to collect their teen-age children. Family and friends couldn't understand why they would want to move to France.

"There aren't any colored folks there." Louise's sister pointed out.

"There are now." said Louise. "The Mulligans will be there. Sister, we can live there, farm there, prosper there, and never have to be afraid that the people around us will punish us for doing well. I will never have to worry there that one of my boys will be brought down, or my girls trifled."

"But you'll be lonely all by yourselves."

"Maybe so." conceded Louise.

"If we don't like it we'll just move back home." added James.

"And what are you going to eat?"

Louise and James started laughing, "Oh we'll make out somehow."

And they took their children and flew to a new life unimaginable to the people at home.

Sylvia and Shep stayed in California, Sylvia was starring in a comedy. Miss Margaret came to stay with them. She had acclimated to the west coast, and Shep and Sylvia loved the oasis of graciousness she created in the house they all shared.

Chance went back to share the summer with Marina. She graduated. A bitter sweet day, two faces missing. She and Chance felt the absence, deeply. A week after the ceremony, Chance decided they needed to celebrate her accomplishment and he threw a party for her at Miss Margaret's. This time they invited Sheriff Ray formally and also the grumpy neighbor. Everyone had a fine night and a headache the next day.

For the rest of the summer Marina continued to help with the swamp study, always hoping to see the white alligator again but he never came back. She did collect a lot of valuable data, bringing to light some animal behaviors, especially across species, which had not been previously recorded.

Chance spent his time canoeing, wind surfing, and doing a little upkeep on Miss Margaret's place. He also supervised the monks and their neighbors, who were renovating the temple house.

One hot and humid afternoon, Chance was out windsurfing and Marina was home writing up her research notes. There was a loud pounding on the door. She looked through the lace curtains of the sidelight window and saw a chubby young man on her doorstep. He was wearing ragged torn clothing and strange sandals that seemed to be home-made. He had a dirty tear-streaked face. He was raising both fists to begin beating on the door again. She opened the door and said gently, "Are you Johnny? I'm Marina." She held her hand out to him. Then she said, "What's wrong? Is something wrong?"

He said harshly, "I don't know you. I want Chance. I want Ten Ha. Where is Mark?" He pushed past her into the house, shouting, "Chance, Ten Ha! Come help Ur!"

"Johnny, please calm down. I can help you. What happened to Ur?"

"I don't know you!" he shouted again. "Where is Chance?" He shoved her aside and looked in the living room. "Chance? Chance? Where are you?" he bellowed.

Marina thought quickly and then said in a firm voice, "I am a friend of Chance. I am a friend of Ten Ha, I am a friend of Johnny and Ur."

Johnny stopped shouting and said to her, "Really?"

"Really and truly." she answered with absolute confidence.

"Where is Chance?" asked Johnny as he calmed down.

"Chance is not here, but I can help you. What is the problem?"

Johnny began crying, loud and hoarse with racking hiccoughing heaves. "Ur is hurt. Ur is shot by a gun."

"Where is Ur?" she asked in an even tone.

"Ur is at my home. Ur and my home. There is blood. I don't know what to do."


When Chance came home, Marina was calling every veterinarian in the area. He heard her say, "I understand. Can you direct to me someone who is willing to treat an injured bear?" There was a pause, then he heard her weary tone, "Okay, thank you very much." Disappointed, she hung up the phone. Johnny burst into the room hollering,

"Chance! Chance! Come help Ur! Ur hurts!"

Marina told Chance that no veterinarian was willing to treat Ur or even attempt the hike into the swamp.

Chance decided to try a different approach. He called their family doctor. "Hello. Dr. Johnston, Chance St. Clare here. No, I'm fine, but a friend of mine has had a terrible accident in the swamp and needs medical attention right away. He slipped with an ax and cut himself pretty badly. Yes, he's bleeding, big wound, some big splinters in the wound, better bring what you need to extract them and stitch him up. No, I don't know how the splinters got there. Yes, he was conscious when his buddy left him to go get help. He's at an old fishing camp. Search and rescue? Oh yeah, I talked to them-they said for me to take you right there, they'll meet us. What's that? I don't know why they decided that. Right, we'll meet you at the town dock in Orange Blossom. ASAP!"

They hurried Johnny out to the car and drove at high speed to the temple. Ten Ha asked no questions when they told him it was an emergency. He just grabbed his satchel and got into the back seat. As they drove rapidly towards Orange Blossom, they explained the situation to him. He put his arm around Johnny's shoulder as Johnny rocked and moaned, sucking on the corner of his shirt.

When they reached the river in Orange Blossom, Chance ran out onto the dock and jumped into the nearest John boat. He checked the fuel level in the tank then fired up the outboard. Johnny cheered up for a moment. " Motor boat ride? Chance has a motor boat?"

"Chance has a motorboat for a day," answered Marina dryly.

Johnny got on board and rocked from side to side a little. "I like this boat of Chance."

Dr. Johnston pulled up in a black sedan and walked down to the boat carrying a very dusty, large black leather medical bag. "It was my Dad's." he said as he swung it aboard. "I just kept it as a souvenir, never expected to put it to use."

Chance backed the boat out into the channel and opened the throttle. Johnny fell backwards from the sudden momentum. With some difficulty Ten Ha and Dr. Johnston, who was a small man, got him back onto his bench seat. Johnny was guffawing the entire time. As soon as he was seated again, he began to cry. Dr. Johnston studied him briefly, looked up and down at Ten Ha in his orange robes, and asked Chance, "Who is this crowd?"

Chance introduced everyone without any explanation of their presence in the boat.

"Ur is hurt." Johnny told the doctor.

"Who is Ur?" asked Dr. Johnston.

"Ur is my friend." answered Johnny.

"Oh, so he's the fellow who was clumsy with the ax."

"No ,"said Buddy, "Ur cannot use a ax. Ur is shot."

"What!" The doctor spun around to Chance. Chance was suddenly concentrating hard on the river ahead and didn't meet his eyes. Marina said, "When Chance called you, he didn't have the full story yet, just a garbled version."

"Not garbled." Johnny corrected her testily. "Johnny is a good boy. Johnny does not tell garbles."

"Well, what is the whole story?" asked Johnston, sounding rather testy as well. "And you did say Search and Rescue is on the way, didn't you?"

"Hopefully." answered Chance. He looked intently at an invisible hazard ahead of them and still didn't meet Johnston's stare.

"So…?" Johnston looked at Marina skeptically over the rims of his glasses.

"So…" she replied."Some kind of hunting accident- someone is shot."

"Where?" he asked.

"At the picnic place." Johnny quickly responded, really pleased to know the correct answer to one of the doctor's questions.

"Where is the wound on his body?" asked Johnston impatiently.

"Here." said Johnny, cupping his hands under the side of his rib cage.

"This is crazy." said Johnston. "He needs to be gotten to the hospital, he needs a surgeon immediately. Why did Search and Rescue tell you to include me?"

Chance and Marina both shrugged and now both of them were busy with the navigation of the John boat, and couldn't talk right then.

Soon Chance found the place on the river where they had tipped the canoe last year. He nosed the boat to the riverbank and tied the painter to a tree root. He and Marina climbed up into the root mat. The doctor handed up his heavy bag; Chance helped him and Ten Ha up to the top of the bank. Johnny pulled himself up and looked around. Dr. Johnston asked, "Where is the fishing camp?"

"My home is this way." said Johnny as he began to walk off into the woods.

"Johnny, wait." Ten Called after him. Johnny stopped. "We have to follow you, we don't know the way."

"Ha ha!" was Johnny's response. "I know! I know where is my home." Then his face fell. "Ur and my's home. I have to go home to Ur now."

He ran off through the woods and disappeared.

They followed in the direction he went, and for a little while could see his wet sandal prints on some of the tree roots. Soon enough, there were no more prints and Marina and Chance were worried.

"How much further?" asked a very sweaty Johnston. "And when the hell is Search and Rescue going to get here?"

Just then they heard Ur roar out in pain. "What the hell was that?" asked Johnston, stopped in his tracks.

"Is a person who is injured." answered Ten Ha, who quickly set off toward the sounds. It wasn't long before they reached the ladder to Johnny's deck. Ur was lying on the deck on his side. Blood was smeared from the ladder to where he lay.

"Jesus! That's a bear!"

"Is your patient." said Ten Ha.

"I don't think so!" replied Johnston.

"Please," pleaded Marina, "Ur is Johnny's family. He needs your help."

"You're out of your mind, you're all crazy!" said Dr. Johnston angrily. "Now get me out of here, take me home!"

"This is home." said Johnny. "Ur is my friend. Ur needs help."

Ten Ha approached Ur and squatted by his side. The bear sniffed his hand and moaned. Ten Ha touched Ur's snout as the bear lay panting, weak from the pain and loss of blood. He was curled up guarding his side and trying not to move.

Ten Ha spoke to Johnny. "We have to get Ur to lie on his back so the doctor can operate."

"The bear will kill me if I try to examine him," said Dr. Johnston.

"Maybe not." said Ten Ha.

Marina asked, "Did you bring any morphine or sedatives?"

"Well yes I did, but I'm not going to try and give a bear an injection. Besides, I'm not a vet and I'm not a surgeon. I have no idea how a bear is going to react to the medications. I don't even know what dosage to give."

Marina said, "I'll give him the injections."

Chance added, "I'd guess he weighs about four hundred pounds. Just figure the dosage like he's a human, a really big human."

"It might kill him." answered Johnston. "And it might make him agitated; drugs can affect animals very differently from people."

"He's going to die if we don't do something." Chance pointed out.

"NO!" screamed Johnny, who then rushed to the bear. Ur opened his eyes and tried to turn his head to see if Johnny was in danger.

Ten Ha said to Johnny, "No, no, Ur will be well. Do not trouble yourself, please. Help Ur be calm and happy, that is how you can help Ur get well."

Johnny sat down at Ur's side and stroked his shoulders gently. Ur closed his eyes and sighed with a shudder.

Dr. Johnston prepared the three syringes and handed them to Marina. "I would jab him in his thigh-in the fleshy part. I can't believe I'm going along with this!" He climbed down the ladder off the deck saying, "I'm getting out of range."

Marina plunged the needle firmly into Ur's flank, who jerked and snarled. She quickly drove the plunger home and leapt back. Ur's eyes were glowing with rage as he whacked at her with his huge black claws, missing her by inches.

"Ur, Ur," crooned Johnny. "Not be mad at Marina. Marina is helping you." The bear turned and looked at Johnny then slumped back to the floor. Marina waited for the sedative to take effect. In about fifteen minutes he seemed to be woozy. She managed to inject the penicillin and more morphine without further resentment from Ur.

While they were waiting for the morphine to take effect, they asked Johnny to tell them more about how Ur was shot.

"We were at the picnic place." Johnny began to cry again as he spoke, "I was finding some good things while Ur waited at the trees. Then a truck came. They cooked meat on the firebox. I said, "Maybe Johnny can have some meat too." The men laughed at me, then shouted some mean names. Ur comes nearer, to see if those bad men were hurting me. The men shouted some more, then one took a gun from the truck and shot Ur. I ran to Ur, Ur cried then we ran away. I helped Ur run slowly until we could not hear those men anymore. Then Ur crawls home, it is so far! Only Ur knows where is home. When Ur and me are home, I know he needs help, so I walk up the river and find Chance."

"How did you get to our house?" asked Chance.

"You give me a paper before when you stayed with Ur and me. You tell me your home is on the paper."

"Can you read, Johnny?" Marina asked him.

"Ho Ho!" laughed Johnny. "No I cannot read-I am not very smart. Because I am not very smart, I walk up the river until I find a road. When I find a road, I find a car with people. I show the paper to the people. First some people say no, and drive their car away from Johnny, but I keep asking people on that road, and then someone says, "Alright, get in." and they bring me to your home."

"That was pretty smart." Chance told him.

Johnny laughed, holding his shaking belly, then said, "Pretty smart for stupid!" and laughed hard again.

Marina said to him, "You must have been very afraid."

He stopped laughing and looked very serious, "I was almost too afraid to go. But Ur needs help. I only know Ten Ha, Chance, and Mark are friends with Ur and friends with Johnny."

When he finished telling the story, Dr. Johnston shook his head wordlessly. The bear was now unconscious. Ten Ha said, "Time to roll bear." They rolled him onto his back with difficulty because of his great weight.

"What do you need?" Chance asked the doctor.

"Well, I'm not sure I'm going near that bear, but if I did, I guess I would shave the area first. You can't see anything with all that fur in the way and it will need to be shaved to clean out the wound and look at the problem."

"I can shave bear." said Ten Ha. "I have experience. Shave monks' furry heads all the time." He had a razor in his bag. He quickly removed the fur in an area around the ugly bullet wound. The sun was setting as they all stared at the puckered, bruised jagged sucked-in hole.

Dr. Johnston instructed, "The next thing is to get some light going and then to probe that wound-see if the bear is all the way under, or if he's still able to respond."

Marina offered to do the initial probing. Dr. Johnston handed her a pair of forceps. She tentatively touched the entry hole. Ur did not move, he just kept breathing deeply and steadily. The doctor prepared a betadine wash and handed the basin to her. "Give it gentle wash, all around the wound."

She did and the bear continued to lie quietly. Chance had a flashlight with him. It provided a little direct light. He gathered dry materials in the woods and made two torches with resinous pine knots. Something Buddy used to make on camping trips, when Chance was a boy.

"That's it for light." he told the doctor.

Johnston said, "Now someone has to try and get that bullet out of the bear."

"I will." answered Ten Ha.

"I suppose you have experience with that too!" sneered Johnston.

"Not with bears." answered the Cambodian monk quietly. There was a shocked silence as they looked at the gentle middle aged monk kneeling by the bear, forceps in his hand. Ten Ha looked at them and said sadly, "No problem." Then he gently inserted the forceps and probed for the bullet. He located it quickly and deftly drew it from the wound.

Johnston approached the sleeping bear now, feeling shamed by the monk's courage. "Let me have a look, see if I can detect what the damage is. I have no idea what a bear's vital signs should be, and I'm absolutely sure that a transfusion is out of the question."

Ten Ha got up and moved to the other side of the bear, ready to assist the doctor. Johnston felt Ur's neck to check the pulse, then he listened through a stethoscope to the bear's heart-beating weak and fast. He heard faint gurgling in the lung on the injured side. The bear's skin seemed cold and clammy.

"There's really no way for me to know what damage has been done to his organs. I don't think his lung is injured. There's no sign of infection yet. I've got quite a bit of penicillin with me. I'll leave it here, and hopefully it will do the trick." He packed the wound with medicated dressing and taped a gauze pad to the skin. "While he's still unconscious let's see if we can get him on a pad or something, and cover him in blankets, try to keep him a little warmer. His skin is awfully cold. He may be in shock.

Once they had gotten the bear onto some old bedding and covered up with some of Johnny's old quilts, Ten Ha said to Dr. Johnston,

"You have done a beautiful act of kindness. I am grateful for the help you have given to us."

"Yeah, well I ought to have you all arrested for kidnapping! I cannot believe you dragged me into this. I ought to have my head examined for having anything to do with it."

"I'm sorry." said Chance. "It was the only way I could come up with to get medical help for the bear. It was an emergency."

"Why don't you take me home." said Johnston grumpily. "I don't want to be here when that bear wakes up."

"Taking the boat on the river at night is a little risky." said Chance.

"So is messing with an injured bear!" snapped Johnston.

"It won't be easy to find the path to the boat in the dark, there are a lot of snakes and alligators around."

"I know where is the boat." said Johnny. Then he had a thought. "But I am staying here with Ur. I am staying here until Ur wakes up."

"I'm not!" reiterated Johnston. He said impatiently to Chance, "Well?"

Chance shrugged and said to Marina, "I'll be back in the morning as soon as I can. Be really careful. As Dr. Johnston mentioned; he is a wounded bear."

"We'll be okay." she said.

They kissed and said good-night. Chance shouldered the doctor's bag and led the way, following the small round shaft of light from his flashlight. Ten Ha watched as their light faded into darkness in the swamp. He suggested that Marina sleep inside the shack and he would keep watch over Ur. She agreed. She fell asleep on the floor and slept lightly, getting up several times to peek out at the deck. Ten Ha kept the pine-knots burning softly through the night. In their feeble glow, each time she looked out she saw Ten Ha seated cross-legged, softly chanting the sutra of loving kindness. Johnny and Ur slept soundly.

At first light, she squatted down next to Ur and watched him closely. His breathing was slow, deep, and rhythmic. She suggested to Ten Ha that it was time for Ur to have another injection of antibiotic. He looked at the peacefully sleeping bear and said, "I will do it."

"No, no, you've done more than your share, watching over him all night. I'll do it!" She held up the syringe, tapping any bubbles to the top and squirting off the top of the liquid. She tapped the bear on the thigh, Ur did not respond. She tapped him harder and still he did not move.

"I wonder if he already has too much morphine in him?" she said.

"I don't know." answered Ten Ha.

"Maybe I should skip it and just give him the penicillin?" she pondered.

"I don't know." Ten Ha repeated. She put the needle deep into the bear's thigh. Ur flew up with a mighty roar and lunged towards her, slicing through her thigh with a monstrous stroke from his clawed paw. Marina drove the plunger home and pulled the needle free of the bear, even as she leapt backwards away from the snarling animal. Blood poured in skirts from the three open stripes in her thigh. Ten Ha leapt toward the bear who was sitting up, as Johnny, who had been sleeping cuddled up to Ur's back, awoke and instantly reached out his hands, stroking the black furry back saying, "Ur is better. Ur is better."

Ur looked at Marina with a bewildered look, as she dropped the syringe and clutched her leg. Ur fell back on the floor, groggy, his head landing in Johnny's lap with a thump. Ten Ha pulled a clean old towel from his satchel as he ran to Marina, telling her to sit down. Almost before she reached the ground, he poured straight betadine into the big bleeding gashes on her lag. She screamed, and then she tried to hold herself together. Ten Ha scrutinized the damage quickly. He promptly wrapped the towel tightly around her thigh. He pressed it hard into two of the wounds, but that was as much area as his hands could cover.

"Can you stay very still and press number three cut?"

"Yes." she said, alert with adrenaline.

"Press down hard and do not move. We want blood to clot. To stop anymore coming."

"Okay."

As they held the increasingly saturated towel tightly to the cuts, she grinned weakly and said,

"Guess that was a really dumb move, huh?"

"Maybe not. Maybe just risky."

"I wish I could say I thought about the risk, then chose to take the chance. The truth is I never thought Ur would hurt me."

"Looks like Ur did not think he would hurt you. Looks like he was surprised in his sleep and acted without thought."

She smiled weakly again, then her teeth began to chatter and she began to tremble.

"You have to master your fear right now." Ten Ha told her. "You have to stay still some more, until bleeding has stopped."

"I can't!" she said as she shook harder.

"You must!" said Ten Ha authoritatively. "You have to control emotions and body or you might die."

Marina was shocked into silence then she began to shake again. "How? How can I control this?"

"It is your fear. Your fear of what has happened. You must tell your mind that danger is over, not happening now, already in the past. Now, everything is pretty much okay, no attack is happening, injury is already present. What you fear is not now, is history, so calm yourself and think only about current problem which is bleeding. Is necessary to stop bleeding, bleeding is now. Mind needs to be in the present and help body now!"

Marina took a breath and concentrated hard on what the monk was trying to convey. Very soon, her trembling stopped, her teeth stopped chattering. The bleeding slowed, then stopped and she said she was cold.

"I know." said Ten Ha.

Johnny had watching, sitting quietly and stroking Ur's head as it lay in his lap. "Ur is in trouble." He said with great worry.

"Maybe not." Ten Ha answered him. "Please get a blanket for Marina."

Johnny laid Ur's head gently on the deck and pulled the top quilt from the pile that covered Ur. He wrapped it tenderly around Marina and said, "I'm sorry Ur hurt you. Ur was bad."

"No," said Marina. "Ur didn't mean to hurt me. He was asleep and didn't know what he was doing. It was my fault."

"No one's fault." Ten Ha gently interjected.

Chance returned in the morning. On his way out the evening before, he barely missed stepping on a small rattle snake on the trail. When he got to the boat, he dislodged a water moccasin and threw it over board, then loaded an equally viperous doctor on board. They chugged slowly, almost blind, back to the town dock in Orange Blossom. As Dr. Johnston stepped on to the dock he said,

"How do you think Ben Hobart is going to feel about the little joy ride we took in his boat, just now?"

"I'm planning to refill the fuel tank, and hopefully he'll never be the wiser."

"You're asking me to leave that out of the story?"

"Actually, I'm asking you to leave the entire story out of the story. I was hoping you would keep all of this to yourself."

"Why would I do that?"

"Because if anyone finds out about this, or even about the existence of Johnny and the bear, their lives will be ruined."

"That boy's life looks like it's already ruination from start to finish. And he certainly isn't fit to look after a wild bear!"

Chance took the time to tell Dr. Johnston the entire story of Johnny and Ur. When he was done, Dr. Johnston said, "Maybe I can concede your point and not say anything about this. But they obviously aren't safe where they are. I mean, look, the bear just got shot. We don't even know if he's going to pull through. Then what happens to Johnny?"

"Yeah," said Chance, "I've been thinking about that. I think maybe we need to start keeping an eye on them. Help them out so they don't have to go out to the state park again."

"It wouldn't hurt that boy to have more social contact. I don't know. I think maybe he should be in supervised care."

"A home, you mean."

"Well, yes. I've treated patients in one a few times." Would you want any friend of yours inside there?"

"Well, no." answered Johnston honestly.

"So will you keep quiet about this and let us see if we can sort things out, try to better the situation?"

"Um, maybe. It definitely goes against my better judgment. I would insist on regular updates. If I don't approve of what is happening, I'll call the authorities right away."

"I guess that will have to do." said Chance as they got into their separate vehicles.

He drove to the film studio and loaded his truck with anything that might be useful. He hitched the boat trailer to his truck and pulled it to the dock. The sun was coming up as he poured gas into the tank of the borrowed boat. He launched his john boat, got the outboard started, and began a tired and apprehensive journey through the dawn and the swamp. When he got to the familiar root, he tied his boat and hoisted some of the cargo onto the bank above him. He included his rifle, which he loaded and slung over his shoulder. Then he tramped his weary way to Johnny's shack. As he climbed the ladder to the deck, he came face to face with pools of fresh blood at eye level as he rose. He saw Ur lying on the deck where he had left him. Then he saw Marina lying on the deck, eyes closed. He thought she was sound asleep. Ten Ha was squatting by the fire, stirring a pot of soup.

"Long night?"

Johnny burst forth loudly with, "Ur hurt Marina!"

Marina's eyes opened and she said, "Oh Chance, I'm so glad you're here."

"What happened?" Chance lifted the quilt covering her. "Jesus Christ!" He pulled his rifle from his shoulder, snarling, "I'll kill that damn bear!" He took aim.

Marina cried out, "No Chance! No!"

Johnny yelled hoarsely, "No! No! No! Not hurt Ur!" and Ten Ha stepped calmly in front of the barrel.

"Get out of my way." Chance hissed at Ten Ha.

"No." said Ten Ha. "No reason to hurt bear. Bear was asleep, surprised. Just acting true to his nature as a bear."

"Well I'm going to act true to my nature, and blow him to from here to yesterday."

Johnny continued to shout loudly, "NO! NO! NO!". Ur woke up drowsily and Johnny bent over his head protectively. Marina spoke in a weak voice. It was hard to hear her over Johnny's shouting. "Chance, listen to me. I don't want Ur harmed. "

"I don't care! That animal attacked you. I'm going to kill him."

"If you do, it's over with us. I will not love you anymore. You will no longer be a person I could care for."

"But Marina, that makes no sense. I need to protect you." He continued to aim the rifle, Ten Ha still standing in front of the barrel.

"I don't want you to protect me when I'm not in danger. Ur's not dangerous. I just made a stupid mistake with him, that's all. What I want from you is that you respect me, and what I care about!"

Chance lowered the rifle. Ten Ha added, "Maybe this can be your true nature."

Johnny whimpered and rocked, patting Ur's forehead who was awake but not moving. Chance sat down next to Marina, holding her hand and stroking her arm.

"Baby, I'm so sorry. I just got so angry when I saw that bloody rag on your leg, I couldn't control myself. I just wanted to destroy the beast who hurt you."

"Well that's you thinking about your feelings." she said simply. "Why don't you start thinking about how the rest of us feel, including Ur. He didn't mean to do this. I stuck him with a needle while he was sound asleep."

Chance hung his head, and then asked, "How badly are you hurt?"

"I think not too bad." Ten Ha answered for her. "She needs wounds sewn up. I did not look very closely, but she can move her toes. Bleeding is stopped. She needs doctor. We must be very mindful when we move her, no bumping. If we bump, she bleeds, maybe a lot."

Marina interrupted him. "If I go to a doctor, they'll kill Ur. Even if I say it is some wild bear, they will hunt some bear down and kill it. Ten Ha, can you sew up my leg?"

"Maybe." replied Ten Ha. "Let me think."

Chance started to protest but Marina raised her hand and said, "Try to think about what is right for me. The right way for me to act. Please try to help me on my path, or at least not obstruct me when I'm already struggling. Try to love me that way, Chance." She was looking deeply into his eyes, and somewhere way inside of himself, he felt something stirring, but he didn't know what it was.

Ten Ha filled a coconut shell with luke-warm broth and carried it to Ur. He sat down next to the bear and began to chant softly. Ur awoke and grunted as he smelled the broth. He pulled himself to a sitting position and Ten Ha held the bowl to his snout. He lapped the broth eagerly, then licked out the bowl.

Marina said, "Looks like he wants some more."

"No more now." said Ten Ha. "We wait. Maybe Ur has damage inside."

"How will you know?" asked Chance.

"There will be a lot of pain."

Ur continued to sit, looking around. He relaxed when he saw Johnny. The bear rose carefully to all fours and padded over to the ladder. Very gingerly, he lowered himself to the ground.

Ten Ha said, "It is better if he stays here, where we can take care of him." The bear waddled slowly and painfully away from the deck.

"Ur! Ur!" Johnny called urgently. "Don't go. Don't go away!"

Ur squatted and took a long pee, groaning and moaning softly. Then he walked slowly back to the ladder and dragged himself back up onto the deck. Ten Ha breezed past him and hopped nimbly to the ground. He went swiftly to the puddle of urine and scooped some into a leaf. He looked at it closely then smiled.

"No blood."

"Is Ur okay?" asked Johnny.

"Maybe." answered Ten Ha. "Tomorrow we will see."

Marina asked Ten Ha again, "Will you sew up my leg?"

"It is risky." said Ten Ha.

"I don't care." replied Marina.

"I care. Risky for you and also risky for me."

"Oh! I didn't think of that. But it is more risky for Johnny and Ur if you don't."

"Yes, I think so." said Ten Ha.

Marina said, "Doc Johnston left a lot of supplies. I think we have what we need."

Ten Ha said to Chance, "You will have to help me. I cannot do this without help."

"What do you want me to do?"

"Hold tools, pass tools, wipe blood, comfort Marina."

Chance turned pale.

"And not faint." added Ten Ha.

"I don't really think this is a good idea."

"Up to you." said Ten Ha.

Marina said nothing, just looked at him steadily, calmly. He knew he was at a crossroad with her. He knew he had done incalculable damage to their relationship by aiming a gun at Ur.

He said to her and to Ten Ha "I get so lost trying to figure out where you are coming from. I want to be where you are, but I just can't see where it is." Marina's eyes began to get a steely look in them. He quickly added, "So I guess I'll fly blind for now." He turned to Ten Ha. "What do you want me to do?"

Ten Ha smiled at him. The smile that then bloomed on Marina's face caused another shift somewhere deep inside of him. His heart pounded faster as he felt a surge of awareness of how much he loved her.

Ten Ha boiled the instruments and needle. He dipped the cat gut into a bath of betadine. He injected a little morphine from a syringe into one of her arms and half a syringe of penicillin into the other.

As he did so, he said, "Sorry, can't give much morphine. Maybe it's better that you stay alert while we are here.", and he glanced around at the swamp.

Then he gently cut and peeled the towel from her wounded leg. Chance gagged when he saw the depth of the meat exposed in her leg. But he held the basin of antiseptic close to her leg and controlled his trembling as Ten Ha swabbed the wounds. Then the monk took a threaded needle and began to sew.

"Does it hurt?" asked Chance with concern.

"Not too much." she said although tears were glistening in the corners of her eyes.

"Hurt later." said Ten Ha quietly as he bent in concentration, calmly and slowly pulling the cat-gut thread through the flesh, pulling the lips of the wound closed and tying a firm knot after each stitch.

"Cut." he instructed Chance, and Chance snipped the thread close to her tender flesh. And so they proceeded- stitch by stitch, knot by knot, until all three gashes were thin puckering lines with ugly black knots of thick thread. Everyone sighed as Chance snipped the last thread. Ten Ha poured straight betadine over the seams of the wounds, then rocked back on his heels, rubbing his neck. Chance wiped beaded sweat from Marina's brow, then wiped his own wet forehead.

Johnny trudged over and looked down. "Your leg is gross." he said to Marina. She burst out in nervous laughter and agreed with him. When he heard her laughing, he began to laugh. Ten Ha sat watching them and soon his shoulders were heaving, too.

Chance watched them in disbelief, then said to Ur, "You and I are the only sane ones around here."

Ur curled his lips back, giving what looked like a grin, and finally Chance began to laugh. He laughed until he cried, then he cried until he began to laugh again. Johnny said, "This is fun!"

"Maybe." said Ten Ha, smiling kindly at the simple man. Then he said to Chance, "It would be good if you take Marina back to town this afternoon. Just in case."

Marina protested but Ten Ha and Chance were firm. They let her rest for a few hours, and then Ten Ha and Johnny handed her down from the deck into Chance's waiting arms. He carried her carefully to the boat. Ten Ha and Johnny walked with him offering to help, but Chance refused to be relieved of the burden.

When they had nestled her into the boat, padded by life-vests, Ten Ha checked his work and was satisfied they had done no damage while moving her.

As the boat pulled away, Chance yelled, "I'll be back in the morning as soon as I get someone to look after Marina while I'm gone."

Ten Ha and Johnny waved and smiled after him as he disappeared up the river.

Ur slept through the afternoon and the night. The following morning, he was nosing around the fire pit, when Ten Ha woke up. "Hungry?" asked the monk. Ur nodded up and down. "I made you some rice porridge yesterday." And handed a pot to the bear.

The bear took it and dipping paw after pawful, devoured all of the gruel in a few short minutes. He looked around for more food, but Ten Ha put a restraining hand on his arm. Ur looked at him and Ten Ha said, "Wait."

Johnny said , "Ur is still hungry. Wants breakfast. Let's get Ur breakfast. Ur always gets my breakfast."

"Must wait. More food maybe will harm him."

"Why?" asked Johnny. "Why wait?"

"Maybe Ur has some holes inside. Maybe food will leak out to wrong places."

"No." said Johnny firmly.

"Maybe." said Ten Ha firmly.

"Oh!" said Johnny. "Ur, you wait. No breakfast now." Ur walked past the two men and climbed slowly down the ladder. He padded painfully away into the swamp.

He returned an hour later with two fish and some bananas. After he laid the food carefully in the cooking area, he collapsed with a "woof" and lay still. Ten Ha approached him slowly, chanting with a soft voice that was somehow also resonating from deep within. He carefully and tenderly inspected the bullet wound. He put his nose close to Ur and sniffed the wound. Ur patted his bald head.

"It's good news!" Ten Ha was smiling broadly.

"What news?" asked Johnny.

"The bullet hole in Ur's side looks good and smells good, also."

"Does not look good," corrected Johnny. "Looks very scary."

"Yes, I agree. But also looks good because there is no blood or pus. And no sweet smell."

"Sweet smell is good." Johnny corrected the monk again.

"Not with a wound," explained the monk. "Sweet smell is infection."

"What is infection?"

"Trouble." answered Ten Ha.

"Oh."


Chance motored slowly back to town. Marina watched the sky and the branches above her, she was relieved to be heading toward help if she needed it.

"I sure wish Buddy was here." Chance said to her with an ache in his voice. "It seems like he always knew just what to do, and how to do it."

"I bet he didn't when he was our age." she told him. "I bet he came by his canniness from knowing the wrong thing to do for a few years."

That idea made Chance feel a little better. "Maybe so, but I sure wish he was here now."

"So do I, Chance, so do I." She sounded forlorn. Then she straightened her back a little and stretched her good leg along the floor boards she was lying on. "Still, you're here and seem to be walking in his footsteps some."

"I think he would have shot the bear." said Chance.

"And I know he would not have."

"How do you know that? How can you be so sure?" He was irritated by her tone of assurance.

"Because he was a man of scope and of vision."

"What! And I'm not?"

"Sometimes not so much. But maybe you're getting there."

"If I didn't have vision, I couldn't make the films I make." he pointed out.

"You have a good eye."

"I don't see what the difference is."

She laughed, "Well, it takes two good eyes to achieve depth perception."

"Clever," he said appreciatively, "but not helpful."

When they reached the boat ramp, Chance backed his truck and trailer down the ramp and loaded the boat with Marina lying in it, in an attempt to jostle her less. He left her curled up in the mass of life jackets and drove slowly, tried to drive softly, the short distance to Miss Margaret's house. He carried her in his arms, and laid her on a day bed in the side parlor. Once she was settled, he telephoned the rest home and spoke to Miss Silvers. She had played one of the nurses in the movie 'Going Om', and had been a strong character on the set. She agreed to take a leave of absence and come work for him, taking care of Marina until she was well. Miss Silvers was an older woman, discrete and caring. She agreed to help spread the tale that Marina had slipped with an axe while splitting wood, although she could clearly see that the wounds were the result of an attack by a large animal. Marina felt sure that she would not gossip with friends or neighbors, and that Johnny and Ur were safe from discovery for a while longer.

The next morning, after Miss Silvers assured him that Marina's leg was doing very well, Chance went back to the swamp, to Johnny's. He found Johnny and Ur napping on the deck and Ten Ha seated in the curl of a big tree root, meditating. Ten Ha told him that Ur seemed to be recovering, and he also said he would stay for two weeks to look after Ur.

They went down to the boat and unloaded fifty pounds of rice and some other supplies. Chance was anxious to get back to Marina.

"I'll be sure someone checks on you every couple of days. Tell them if there is anything you need and I'll send it to you. And.... ," he paused and then said, "Thanks for everything."

"You are welcome." said the monk. "Please bring Tara to stay with Marina. She would be fine at the temple, the monks are very warm with her, but Marina will be more cheerful if she has Tara to keep her company."

Over the next few weeks Marina and the bear mended, Marina more quickly than the Ur, but Ur seemed to have some natural sense of his physical limitation, so didn't re-injure himself or slow his own healing. Ten Ha returned to the temple and resumed his duties. Tara also went back to the monks and was joyful to be reunited with him. She danced her funny stiff-legged hop and oinked in her chowish voice.

Everyone involved in the adventure agreed that from now on, Johnny and Ur should have some regular friendly support. Chance found an elderly man in Orange Blossom who spent most of his mornings fishing on the river from a john boat. He was a quiet widow-man, his children all grown and gone away. Miss Margaret was consulted in a phone call. She had known him all her life, and was firmly of the opinion that Mr. Sharon was the proper man for the job of keeping track of Johnny and Ur. Chance, Ten Ha and Marina all went along to introduce Mr. Sharon to his new charges. They were reassured to find him matter-of-fact with both Johnny and the bear, who each accepted his presence without resistance. When they explained the plan to Johnny, he burst into a big sunny grin.

"I don't like that picnic place anymore. Now Ur can be safe and not go there anymore."

They left man and bear waving on the riverbank and as they motored back to Orange Blossom Mr. Sharon said, "I've seen a lot of queer things in my life, but this beats all." He looked at Ten Ha, glanced down at his orange robe and asked, "Is this the way they do things in your part of the world?"

"No." said Ten Ha. "No black bears in Cambodia."

Marina and Chance accompanied Mr. Sharon on his first few visits to Johnny, until it was clear that he was accepted there and that he was no threat to the simple man or the bear. Mr. Sharon was glad to have someone who needed him and something interesting to do while he was on the river. And, he never told anyone about Johnny or the bear.

Early on during Marina's recovery, Chance offered to pay for a plastic surgeon. He was concerned about the scarring on her leg.

She gave him a little crooked quizzical smile and said, "Are you kidding! These three stripes are my talisman. Like tracks of a lightning strike. That was a big event!" Then she asked curiously, "Does the scar bother you? Do you find it repulsive?"

"Not at all." he said as he bent over and kissed each of the three stitched grooves. Everything about you is sexy- even your sexy scars."

"I'm really glad you feel that way."

He took her in his arms and kissed her slowly and softly. Then as she responded, he kissed her deeply. He rocked her, surrounded her, melted her. She felt wave after wave of desire, tenderness, fulfillment.

"Will you marry me now?" he asked as they coasted to shore.

Her own hesitations, the memory of Grace's words; all were washed away in her spent passion, and she said,
"Yes."

They lingered for several days enjoying the new softness they had found in each other. Then they called Shep and Sylvia in California to tell them that a marriage was imminent. Shep answered the phone and when he heard the news, all he said was,

"Can I call you back in about an hour?"

"Sure." Chance was nonplussed by his friend's response. Marina was on the extension line. She hung up and came into the hall.

"Well, that was anticlimactic. What's that about?"

In about forty five minutes the phone rang. Shep and Sylvia were both on the line.

"How about if we join you for the wedding?" asked Shep, a little breathlessly.

"I'm counting on you being the best man!" Chance said testily.

"Nope," said Sylva, "You'll have to do better than that. We want to join you at the altar, double wedding."

"Yeah." added Shep, "I had to ask Sylvia first."

"Ask her to marry you?" Marina sounded incredulous.

"Yep."

"As long as it's in Orange Blossom, I'll come join in." said Sylvia merrily.

The two couples decided the sooner the better. Chance, because he didn't want Marina to change her mind; Marina, because she had made up her mind; and Shep and Sylvia, because they hoped that a shorter time for preparations might limit the invasive publicity. Miss Margaret required two months to get the house in order- they gave her six weeks. Everyone agreed that autumn would have the sweetest weather for a wedding.

Sylvia still had a month of shooting in Hollywood but Shep and Miss Margaret arrived a few days after the phone conversation.

Miss Margaret put the men to work on the old house, "You two are only going to be in the way, otherwise. The groom serves no purpose except on the actual day of the ceremony, for an hour or two. All you have to do then is not stumble with foot, tongue, or hand. And hopefully provide the ring at the sanctified moment. In the meantime why don't you freshen up the paint on the trim on the front of the house."

The young men regarded her as the ultimate authority on etiquette and social niceties; also, they were relieved to be excused from the plans and arrangements. Since Miss Margaret seemed determined to be the wedding director, the two brides conferred together and decided not to struggle against her torrent of determination.

Sylvia was of the opinion the less theatre the better. Talking with Marina on the phone, she said, "I'd like this to just be a real day. I've been working in the land of artifice and fanfare; I'd just as soon keep my marriage vows in a whole nother world. Do you have your heart set on a great big do, Sugar?"

"Not a one bit. I'm with you all the way!"

"Where are going for your gown?" Sylvia asked her.

"Some bridal shop downtown-something off the rack."

"Would it drive you crazy to wait til I get there, and we girls could just go down together and pick out our dresses, no fuss, no bother?"

Marina started laughing. "I think that would be just fine."

"What about a photographer, Honey?"

"What about one?"

"What if we just didn't have any pictures? What if we just had one real day, and remembered it in our own little bitty minds? What if we just had a real day; right in the moment?" Marina hesitated. Sylvia said hurriedly, "Now if you want all the trimmings, I understand. It was just an idea, I'm not wedded to it!"

"No, no, I kind of like it. I'm just wondering what the two cinematographers are going to say. You know, they're getting married that day, as well."

"I know. Isn't it a remarkable coincidence. Think how frustrated they may be, not being able to film themselves. It's kind of delicious to contemplate."

Both women were giggling into the phone.

"Minister?" asked Marina.

"Oh, Miss Margaret will get hers from the Methodist church there in town, but can we have the ceremony at the house?"

"Sure!" answered Marina. "Bridesmaids, groomsmen, flower girls?"

"Well, I'd like to pass on all that except for the flower girls. I do like the little girls in white dresses strewing flower petals-lots of flower petals."

"Me too," said Marina happily. "Now the big question: what's the cake going to be?"

"Whatever you want Sweetie, just go wild with it!"

"Flowers?"

"Lots and lots of them."

And so Miss Margaret hired a little army of helpers, and with their help, she transformed her beautiful old house into a flowering wonderland.

When Sylvia arrived from the West Coast, the two prospective brides went to the city and walked into the first bridal shop they spotted. Each picked out a gown within twenty minutes. They had to bribe the shop keeper to do the fittings on the spot. They asked to have the dresses ready in five days. The man said he could do it, but it was not the way in which he was accustomed to doing business. Sylvia slipped him a hundred dollars, winked and then gave him her most gracious smile. He melted into a puddle as the two friends walked out the door.

The wedding was as smooth as raw silk. Miss Margaret invited practically the whole town. The two couples invited their friends from near and far. James, Louise and several young Mullicans came from Provence, shining, boisterous, prospering. Mark and Marie came to give Marina away. Everyone came from Ten Ha's temple, including a troupe of little girls who danced a Cambodian folkdance gracefully and sweetly, looking like little pastel flowers as they moved.

Tara, the Chow dog, was an invited guest but she ran everywhere getting between people's legs and under the feet of anyone with food.

Miss Margaret said to her, "I'm not going to fuss at you, but I expect you to settle down. Otherwise, I will have to ask you to leave."

Tara paid no attention, and had to be escorted to a back bedroom for the remainder of the festivities.

No stars or entities from Hollywood were on the guest list, so the press and Sylvia's publicity mangers remained ignorant until after the day was done.

The two couples were wed without pomp, in a beautiful gathering. In the softening evening, a hundred couples danced under the stars, while the local band played the same old songs that were always played. People went home satisfied that they had helped weld the seams of two new families in their midst. Chance and Marina floated home to their little bungalow in the city; while Sylvia and Shep sought their bower on the third floor of the gracious old house.

Miss Margaret was up early the next day, sipping tea amid a wonderfully disheveled and flower strewn loggia. After a while, the local people she had hired to put it all together, arrived to clean it all up. They had been guests at the celebration, so were a bit relaxed and hung over, but no one was in a rush.

Over the next few years, Marina worked as a research assistant at the University. She directed the field study in the swamp, and published several significant articles chronicling hitherto unseen behaviors in a number of the species she observed. The interspecies observations were particularly exciting and her name became known in select academic circles.

When Chance was home, he continued to film some of the animals she studied. He was away for several months at a time, making movies with Shep. Thanks to Marie's business and marketing abilities, Spanish Moss Productions thrived and grew, remaining independent in spite of several tempting offers from the large studios.

Sylvia also remained independent, making another Hollywood film. When she and Shep decided to have a child, Chance and Shep wrote a screenplay with a starring role for her as a pregnant woman. Its setting was the beach, so they were all able to be together in Orange Blossom for months. Whenever Marina got a break at work, she joined them on the beach where they were filming. Sylvia's body began to show her pregnancy in October. They filmed through the winter and into the migrating spring.

The movie told a story of a young married woman who had not intended to get pregnant. She was busy with a career as a sales executive, and didn't want the distraction. She was angry about the invasion in her body. And angry with her husband who was over-joyed but had no intention to be involved in childrearing.

In the story, she rents a house on the beach for the winter and retreats, wanting to be alone to think things out. There are very few people and at first it seems desolate and lonely to her, but she feels this outer world is an appropriate reflection of her inner sour mood.

When she arrives, the ocean is warm enough and she swims every day, the crashing waves pushing her and thrusting her over the sand. She feels her anger manifested, and begins to take joy in the outward expressiveness that nature is giving to her. She walks for hours down the desolate strand. Every day as she looks around, she sees more and more life around her that she had overlooked in earlier days. She begins to recognize the flocks of birds, the rabbits in the sea grapes on the dunes. Day by day, quiet night by quiet star-filled night, her heart opens to the rhythms of the baby within her: the same rhythms of the sea and all the life around her. She emerges in the spring, swollen with promise, her heart harmonized with her world. She returns home to her husband, where her changes cause a change in him and he is drawn into the circle of her new perspective, opening doors between them.

Sylvia became more and more radiant as the months progressed. Chance and Shep made an exquisitely beautiful film of an exquisitely beautiful, voluptuous woman. Some of the filming of the winter beach looked almost monochromatic until the camera zoomed in and lingered on individual birds, animals or fall flowers. Then the subtle colors seemed to saturate before the viewers eyes. It was another example of Chance's unique vision through the lens. They called the film 'The Sea Change'. The critics panned it but the filmgoers loved it. It was a huge hit at independent theatres, thanks again to Marie's brilliant marketing.

The next two years passed in a whirl for everyone. Sylvia took a break from film, enjoying raising her little girl at home in Orange Blossom. Shep worked on old projects in the can, and stayed present and very much in the life of his wife and tiny daughter. Chance worked on some small independent projects which took him to many parts of the globe for short periods of time. Marina continued to work on the field study in the swamp. Two years of acute observation led to her proposing some startling and controversial concepts in animal behavior.

Dr. Tamlin, the professor in charge, turned the study entirely over to Marina and took a leave of absence. He and Marina had become close friends over the years. He was astute in the world of biology although considerably less so in the world of day to day. He valued the quality of her mind and perceptions. He said that it was high time that she assumed the reins and receive the credit for the study. He followed a grant to Northern California to study two young dolphins. The dolphins had been captured by La Pacifica, and the park was given a permit to keep them in captivity for the duration of Dr. Tamlin's research. He studied vocalization, identifying language patterns in their communication with each other. He kept in close touch with Marina, advising her on her work and helping her develop several more behavioral theories on intraspecial cooperation.

Her interest in the work grew as she went deeper and deeper in her levels of understanding of the forest and the swamp around her. She found herself reacting to the changes in the birds' songs, frequently recognizing by their signaling, that a predator was arriving in the glade. She could distinguish their calls well enough to know what animal was about to appear: a snake, a raccoon, a raven. Soon she realized other animals understood and were using the birds' warnings, as well.

She trained a number of students to run the study, and eventually she was able to travel with Chance sometimes and also to visit him on location for several weeks at a time. It was a good life. Both of them were striving hard in the fields of their separate passions. Periodically Chance asked her to give up her career so they could be together more of the time, but she always quietly but firmly refused.

"I don't see what you can have left to learn out of that one little patch of the world!"

"The longer I look, the more I see."

"What? Microbes?"

"No," she smiled good-humoredly. "Levels upon levels of behaviors and interactions."

"Don't you get bored?"

"Sometimes. Then I come see you."


Dr. Tamlin returned to Florida, but Marina remained director of the now famous study. He spent his days in his office, writing up his notes from the dolphin project. One day Marina met him there for a meeting. She found him in tears.

"The dolphins." he cried.

"Has something happened to them?" she asked.

"La Pacifica is refusing to release them. They are claiming the dolphins have been habituated to humans and can't safely be returned to the wild."

"Oh no!" Marina paled. "Can't you fight them on that? You're the authority. Surely they can't override your call on this?"

"There's a meeting with Fish and Wildlife out there but I can't go. My brother is critically ill-I have to stay here. Those dolphin trusted me-they're like my children." He put his grey-haired head on his desk and wept. Marina wanted to pat him on the back, but he'd always been so stern and hard-shelled that she refrained. After a few seconds he sat back up, blew his nose in handkerchief, and wiped his eyes behind his rimless glasses.

"I'm sorry to make such a display of myself. I didn't mean to trouble you. I'm surprised myself at how strong my feelings are."

"It's okay. I understand. I would feel the same way. Could I look after your brother while you went out there?"

"No, he's really in crisis. I have to be here. I have no choice."

"What if I went? Could I represent you?"

"Of course you could!" He brightened. "You'd probably be a lot more persuasive than me. I don't think public presentation is really my forte."


Marina asked Chance to go with her, but he and Shep were in the middle of putting a soundtrack together for a film they were working on, and he didn't want to break his concentration. So she flew alone to the west coast, rented a car, and found a hotel by the ocean.

In the morning she went to see the dolphins at La Pacifica, the marine park. They were in a small aquatic pen, a holding tank made of concrete, cordoned off from a larger pool. The big pool was used to train marine animals for the La Pacifica shows. As she approached the small tank, she could see the two young dolphins lying listlessly bored on the surface. She spoke to them and both heads jerked up, as they whistled and clicked. They came to the edge and lifted their heads until their long jaws were resting on the edge of the pool deck.

"Hello my darlings." she murmured as she stroked first one forehead and then the other. She sat down and put her feet into the water so they could smell her scent and know who she was. The water was dirty and oil floated on the surface. "Oh my lovely friends," she crooned, "Don't worry, we'll have you out of here soon."

The dolphins made purring sounds and nodded their noses into her hands, while nudging her legs. They slipped back into the water and made a mad happy circle in their tiny confines, then they raised their heads in unison and clicked wildly. They came back to her and nuzzled her feet. She left reluctantly and the two animals cried out softly and helplessly as she walked away.

The next day she attended the meeting held at the National Fish and Wildlife offices. She walked into the meeting, looking seriously professional. She was wearing a skirted pin-striped business suit that Marie had air-shipped to her from Manhattan. She found two marine biologists from La Pacifica had arrived before her and were in chummy conversation with the wildlife official. The three men were in a rowdy conversation about last night's basketball game on television. The federal official nodded at her as she sat down, his attention never leaving the conversation. After a few minutes they wound down and he turned to Marina and said, "And who might you be, little lady?"

"I'm Marina Francis, sent by Dr. Tamlin."

"And who is Dr. Tamlin?" he asked in a faintly derogatory tone.

"He's the guy that wants to see the dolphins released." One of the biologists answered for her.

"Thanks Ted. How is this any of his business?"

Ted replied, "He's the professor who was doing some research with the dolphins."

"What's his beef?" asked the official, still speaking to Ted. He had turned his chair to face Ted and now had his back to Marina.

Marina said loudly, "Has this meeting officially opened?"

He turned back around to her, "No, but I'll open it right now, on the subject of continuing the permit of La Pacifica for maintaining two dolphins already at their facility."

"The permit is held by Dr. Tamlin." Marina corrected him tersely.

"Well, we'll just transfer it over to La Pacifica."

"No you won't!" Marina's eyes were blazing. "I request permission to read Dr. Tamlin's statement and enter it into the minutes."

The official looked at his watch. "Is this going to take very long? I have a meeting with the District Commissioner."

"No, it's not very long." snapped Marina. She read the two pages outlining the procedure for safely releasing the two young dolphins back into the wild by gradual acclimation from the bay immediately in front of La Pacifica. The plan included netting off a portion of the bay to house the two dolphins until they had integrated into one of the wild pods in the area.

"What do you think, Don, Ted?" The official quizzed the La Pacifica biologists.

"Oh, just a bunch of airy-fairy academia," replied Don. "It'd be nice if things worked that way, but these animals have been way too habituated to captivity. They're too vulnerable to ever release into the wild."

The federal official looked at Marina and said, "Well?"

"Well," she responded, "What an amazing coincidence that La Pacifica should harbor this opinion so shortly after new restrictions on capturing wild dolphins have caused a shortage in their collection of performing animals, and at a time when their captive breeding program is proving a total failure."

"I hope you're not implying that we are acting out of any motive of gain." said Ted in an aggressive tone.

"I'm not implying, I'm stating it outright." retorted Marina coldly.

"Now young lady!" cautioned the official.

"Don't you "young lady" me, you patronizing weasel!" she instantly replied.

"Dolphins stay at La Pacifica, hearing closed!" said the official coolly. He turned back to Ted and took up the subject of basketball again.

Marina stood up angrily. "It doesn't end here. I'll appeal this to whoever is above you!"

"No appeal process. My decision is final." He smiled at her. She was determined to shed no tears. She looked at him coldly and said,

"We'll see." Then she walked out, to the sound of three men laughing at her back.


She was still burning with rage when she reached her hotel room. She sat on her balcony, angry tears of frustration spurting from her eyes as she looked out over the grey sea rolling its endless small waves up onto the rattling pebble beach. When she was calmer, she called Dr. Tamlin to relay the grim news.

"Surely we can appeal?" she asked him. "They said we can't, but surely we can!"

"We can," he responded in a heavy tone, "and we will; but the appeal process will drag on and on. It often takes years to get a decision."

"Well we can't leave those dolphins there suffering for years."

"We don't really have much choice."

"Sure we do! What do you think their chances would be if we just release them straight away into the bay?"

"Actually, they would probably do pretty well, barring misfortune. They haven't been in captivity very long. There's even a fairly good chance that they can find their original family pod. La Pacifica captured them there in the bay. But we don't have the authority to do that."

"So? What do you think is in their best interest?"

"Releasing them, obviously."

"Then let's do it."

"How?"

"Hide in the restrooms until after closing time, then somehow get the gate open to the beach and get them down the stairs and across the rocks to the water.

"That would be almost impossible without equipment and a lot of manpower."

"'Almost' is the operative word here. We have to try."

"Marina, I really want to, but I cannot leave my brother. He's barely holding on and he needs me here. I'm sorry but I can't do this."

She could hear the pain in his voice and knew the choice was pulling him in two. "It's okay; I'll find someone to help."

"Be careful! And won't they know it was you? You'll be arrested. It will be a federal offense, you could go to prison!"

"I'll cover my tracks."

As soon as she hung up, she dialed again, "Chance, Chance, I need your help!"

"Baby, what's the matter, are you alright?"

"Yes, I'm fine. I need your help with the dolphins. The meeting went badly. They're not going to be released. I'm going to break them out of La Pacifica and set them free. I need you here right away to help me."

"Whoa there! Honey, that is Crazy talking. You can't just steal two dolphins. We'll buy them, then let them go. Calm down now, you're not thinking clearly."

"I am! They can't be sold, they belong to the federal government. La Pacifica can keep them because they have been granted a permit, but they can't be sold."

"Oh honey, I'm so sorry. I'm sorry about the dolphins."

"Don't be sorry, get on a plane and come help me."

"Baby, I can't. you know that."

"You mean you won't. Chance, I'm begging you. I need you here. Now! I really need your help."

"Baby, I can't. I can come in a week. Shep and I are on an amazing roll with the sound track. I can't break that off."

"Yes you can. This is more important. Chance, I've never insisted, never interfered. Set it aside and do this for me."

"Honey, I can't. I'm sorry. I'll come in a week."

"It has to be done sooner than that. I'm sure La Pacifica is going to pull my pass in the next couple of days and I won't have access to the private area where they are.

It has to be done tomorrow or the next day. They weigh so much I can't possibly move them without help."

"Baby, I'm sorry."

She hung up the phone without another word. Then she called the Buddhist temple. She knew Ten Ha would not speak on the phone so she asked the Cambodian woman who answered to act as a go between. "Please ask him if he will come to California now, to help me save two dolphins."

"Two what?" The woman didn't understand much English.

"Two big fish."

"Okay. Just wait a minute." Marina heard her speaking in Cambodian, then heard Ten Ha respond in the background.

The woman said, "He says 'yes'. How can he come there?"

Marina thought quickly. "Can someone there drive him to the airport and buy him a plane ticket?"

"Just wait a minute please." said the woman. More muffled conversation, then the woman came back on the line. "He says 'yes'. Temple has money. My husband will bring him now."

"Thank God!" breathed Marina.

"Excuse me?" asked the woman.

"Thank you." answered Marina.

"You're welcome." said the woman in an automatic sing-song voice, and then she hung up before Marian could discuss the details of time of flights. She called the airport and got the schedule of planes arriving with Florida connections. Next she booked two tickets home for the following day. She splashed some water on her face, then drove to La Pacifica to survey the scene and plan the escape.

The dolphins were delighted to see her. They crowded onto the pool deck and stuttered and clicked excitedly. She rubbed their heads and spoke gently to them. Ted, the marine biologist from the meeting, walked up behind her and said, "See, it's not that bad, is it."

"I wouldn't want to live in that water." she replied. "It's filthy, and this pool is way too small to house them. How can you keep them like this?"

"They're fine." he said dismissively. "Besides, they'll be training and performing in the big pool a lot of the time. They'll be too tired to care when they're in here."

She just shook her head and went back to stroking the dolphins.

"They really like you. You should apply for a job here."

"Yeah right." she said.

When the dolphins wiggled back into the water, Marina asked where the nearest restroom was. She waited inside until Ted left the area, took a careful look around, and then left the park. At her hotel, she sat on the balcony watching the ocean and the sky. She remained sitting outside in the dark, after the sun had settled for the night below the horizon line.

In Florida, Ten Ha asked the helpful woman at the temple to place a phone call to Chance at the studio in Orange Blossom. He relayed the message in English, through her.

"He say, please go California. Marina need you."
Chance said, "Tell him I can't, not this week."
'He say, please. He think you will want to."
Chance was surprised. "Does he understand how busy I am right now?" Shep was sitting in a chair next to him at the board where they were working on the sound track. Chance looked over at him, with a perplexed look. He cupped the phone and whispered, "It's someone from the temple, calling for Ten Ha."

Shep looked at him curiously, while the woman on the phone was saying, "Yes, you very busy. Ten Ha say busy not important. Marina busy too, more important you help Marina."

"I'm sorry he sees it that way. I understand his concern for the dolphins."

A pause while she repeated this to the monk. Then, "He is concerned for you, not dolphins. It is your suffering. Best for you, best for Marina, you go help her now."

"I appreciate his concern. Tell him 'thanks'. I'll go at the beginning of next week. Bye now." He hung up the phone.

"What was that all about?" asked Shep.
"Ten Ha was insisting I go out to California."
"Ten Ha never tells people what to do."

"I know. Strange."
"Are you going?"
"Next week. When we're finished."
"I think you should go now." Shep looked at him earnestly.
"Not you too? We are right at the sweet point to have this whole score come together."

Sylvia walked in, holding Baby May. She overheard part of the conversation, and as she rocked her daughter on her knee she said, "If you don't go, you're an idiot. An ungrateful idiot."

"What's that supposed to mean?" Chance was irritated. "You're an artist, you know how critical it is to stay with the flow when the creative juices are really on."

"Where the hell do you think those juices are coming from?" she retorted. "Those people who love you so much, who have believed in you, supported you. The way they live their lives is what you're feeding on, that's the juice that makes you great as an artist. They have inspired you by who they are. And they have been there for you. Marina needs your help-that's the creative flow right now!"

When she finished Shep nodded in agreement. "It's important to be there for them when they really need you."

"That may be so, but for me to spin a film to wholeness, I cannot break my concentration. I have to keep focused. I have to choose that sacrifice. As you know, that commitment is the price that comes with the gift, if you're going to honor it."

Sylvia put her lips together and said, "Pffff!" and then left the room carrying Baby May with her.

"That's a couple of hard-headed women we're tied up with." Chance appealed to Shep.

Shep was watching his wife depart, her regal back splendid in anger, stern with indignation. His daughter gazed at him placidly over her mother's shoulder, smiling, dreamy and content. "Also couple of warm hearted women. You should listen to her, man. She's right."

Chance looked at him long and hard, then turned back to the mixing board. The two men continued to work side by side, but Shep thought to himself that the creative flow had up and left the room.

Marina's mind raced all night: planning, scheming, worrying as she tried to think her way through to a successful ending of the coming day. She was exhausted when dawn at last began to illuminate the ocean outside her window. She hoped Ten Ha would arrive on the noon flight. She paced all morning in her room and on her balcony, until finally it was time to drive to the airport, an hour away. She stood in the terminal watching the plane disgorge its passengers, but no orange figure emerged. She stood watching after the last passenger came down the ladder and walked across the tarmac. Her heart sank. She found a pay phone and called the temple, but no one answered.

It was midafternoon and soon it would be too late to take the first steps of her plan to free the dolphins. She went to La Pacifica alone to begin the process. She knelt over the dolphin pool. It was dirtier and smellier than the day before. The two animals sang their chirps of welcome and hope. As she knelt, one of them rose up and gently bumped her charm necklace as it dangled over the pool. She leaned back and fingered the two golden dolphin charms that had lain next to her skin for several years, since the white alligator had presented them for her. "Surely," she thought, "surely this is meant to succeed."

She walked over to the gate leading to the narrow rocky shore and the sea a short distance beyond. She leaned over the gate and tossed her watch onto a rock a few feet away. Then she went looking for a security guard.

"Excuse me, I've lost my watch."

"Lost and found is next to the entrance gate." he said.

"No, I mean I've dropped my watch while I was sitting on that stone wall over there. Dropped it on the rocks."

"Oops." said the guard as he looked over the wall. "I'll open the gate and you can go down and get it. Be careful, those rocks can be pretty slippery."

He turned the key in the lock and held the gate open for her. She walked lightly down the dank stairs, over a few rocks, and retrieved her watch.

"Is it still working?" asked the guard. She held it to her ear as she came up the stairs.

"I'm not sure. What do you think?" She handed the watch to him as she passed the edge of the gate. He held the watch to his ear, looking out into the distance as he concentrated on listening for a ticking sound. In the brief instant that he was distracted, she slapped the little piece of duct tape she had hidden in her hand, over the tongue of the lock to keep it from latching. She whipped a wad of bubble gum, sticky as goo, out of her mouth and stuck it over the duct tape. She closed the gate and turned her back on the guard pretending to turn the key in the lock.

After she handed the key back to him, he said, "I think you got lucky, it seems to be working."

"That's great. This may be my lucky day." As he began to tug lightly on the gate to be sure it was latched, she said very sweetly, "You have been so helpful."

He stopped what he was doing and turned to look her over. "My pleasure."

He winked at her and strolled away. She returned to the dolphin's pool and whispered to them, "Tonight, tonight."

She returned to the airport at three in the afternoon, to meet the only other flight that day. She melted with relief when she saw a robe clad man holding a furled umbrella and a small orange shoulder satchel. She almost hugged him as he came through the door. He smiled warmly and asked no questions as they walked out to the car. Marina said, "I knew I could count on you."

Once they were seated in the car, before she turned the engine on she said, "We could be arrested for freeing these animals. It will be considered theft. You could go to prison."

"Or be deported." added Ten Ha.

"Oh God! I never thought of that." she said in horror. "Oh Ten Ha! I can't ask you to do this for me. I've been so thoughtless. I'll figure out how to do it myself."

"Not doing for you." He said gently. "Doing for two other beings, the dolphins."

"But still, the risk is too great."

"No. Great, but not too great. Sometimes act of compassion brings suffering to oneself. It is important to understand possibility of consequences to oneself. Also important to know true nature of suffering."

"I don't know what you mean."

"Is okay. No problem. You ready now?"

"Yes." She replied as she started the engine. As they approached the hotel she asked him to duck down, and when she got out of the car she asked him to lie across the seat, out of sight.

"It's better if we are not seen together. If no one sees you with me, you may not be a suspect when the dolphins go missing."

He kept quietly out of sight, looking like a rumpled orange sheet to anyone who might have glanced into the parked car. She retrieved her luggage from the room and checked out, making a point of telling the hotel clerk that she was flying home that evening. When she got back in the car, she reached onto the back seat, retrieved a bulky brown jacket and handed it to Ten Ha .

"Put this on, so your robe isn't so obvious, it's like a beacon. We need to go someplace where we won't be noticed, until it gets dark enough to go over to La Pacifica."

She drove north on the highway, past La Pacifica and then along the palisades looking over the grey blue sea. They pulled into overlooks and savored each scene of wild crashing beauty until another car came along. Then they drove away before anyone got a good look at the two of them. Finally as the sun was sinking they traveled back south, winding the curves of the coastal highway. They discussed details of how they would proceed. She drove past the entrance to La Pacifica and turned right half a mile further on. She had scouted this little lane and knew it ended in a cul de sac. She parked at the end of the road, then they walked for a few minutes through the pine woods to a rock strewn beach. The last glimmer of light was fading.

The moon was rising over the trees and they were able to see, as they walked the half mile to the sea wall that bounded La Pacifica. Marina climbed the slippery steps and pushed hard on the gate. The gum gave way promptly and the gate swung open. The dolphins heard them coming across the concrete deck. They chortled and whistled softly. Marina and Ten Ha went to get a rescue stretcher at the big performance pool. Marian had noticed it earlier in the day, and she was relieved to find that it had not been locked up somewhere for the night.

As they carried the stretcher to the dolphin's pool they heard a knocking sound coming from a small aquarium built into a wall. A medium sized octopus was pushing and tapping on the lid from the inside. The top was latched on the outside, so he struggled in vain. He saw them and pressed his tentacles against the glass, waving to them and watching them with his luminescent eyes. Ten Ha raised his palm toward the octopus, greeting him. The octopus raised one tentacle tip in response, and then flushed a sad white strumming color over his whole body, like a hopeless ghost-wave of northern lights. Ten Ha swiftly flipped the latch of tank open, and then hurried on with Marina to do the work they had come do.

They laid the stretcher longwise, one end right on the pool's edge. Ten Ha stroked the animals' snouts, speaking to them in his native tongue. The dolphins were calm. They sighed softly. Marina patted the canvas of the stretcher and coaxed, "Come on, hop up, come on, up here."

The dolphins clicked, urgently staccato, as they swam in a fast circle. Then one of them leapt out of the water and landed squarely on the stretcher. He seemed to laugh as he lay there. Both dolphins were less than two years old. Even so, they weighted about two hundred pounds each. Marian and Ten Ha took hold of the handles at the far end of the stretcher and with immense effort hauled it with the dolphin in it, to the head of the stairs. The dolphin left behind cried with distress.

"One moment." Said Ten Ha. He reached into his satchel for a pair of scissors and cut three long wide strips from the bottom of his robe. They bound the strips carefully and firmly around the dolphin to harness him in. Then standing behind the stretcher, they slid it slowly, carefully, down the steps to the beach. Marina felt something pulling, then tearing, then giving way in her back. She stifled a groan and forced herself upright. It took them at least an hour to drag and maneuver the first dolphin across the beach to edge of the water. They dragged the stretcher into three feet of water and untied the strips of cloth. The dolphin slid into the clean ocean water that was the mother element to him. He squealed and rolled in the water. Then he began calling to the one still trapped in the pool. The captive animal cried out to her cousin with a voice full of fear and longing. Marina could barely force herself back up the stairs, the pain in her back and down her leg was demanding that she stop, but she pushed herself on. The dolphin in the tank leapt promptly onto the stretcher, knowing it was the path to freedom. Ten Ha tried to pull the loaded stretcher by himself, but he could not.

"Maybe we have done what we can do."

"No," she said, "we are too close. I can't not finish this."

She pushed the pain away from her mind and forced her muscles to haul the second animal across the deck, down the stairs and across the beach to the sea. She could not bend down to help Ten Ha release the ties. Once the second dolphin was free Ten Ha told Marina to lie on the stretcher on the beach and rest for a little while. He would be right back.

"We have to get out of here." she told him.

"There is something I must do." he said as he hurried back up the stairs. She lay down and watched for him, fretful to see the first hint of dawn coming over the tree tops. She was glad to see him return quickly. He had the octopus riding on his shoulders as he walked past her into the cold water. The octopus slid down his chest, and once in the water it held onto the monk's forearm with two tentacles. He looked into the man's eyes with his own great curious eyes, and then thrummed a series of pastel colors across its upper body, while taping rhythmically on Ten Ha's inner wrist. Ten Ha smiled down at it and said, "Go in peace, my friend."

The octopus released him, folded all eight legs up to short little legs and jetted away into the still inky night-filled ocean. The wine-colored water was reflecting the early morning rose-fingered sky.

Marina could not walk. Her back had given all there was to give. Ten Ha pulled her into the water and holding her collar, towed her behind him as he walked into water up to his waist. He turned and began to wade in the direction of the car, towing her the entire way. They were both cold and exhausted when they left the water and reached the path through the woods. She put her arm over his shoulders and he staggered as he helped her make her way up the trail

Ten Ha had never operated an automobile, so it was up to Marina to drive. She gripped the wheel with both hands. She was wracked with pain. She had no sleep for two nights and had not eaten since yesterday.
"I wish Chance were here." she said miserably.
"Yes." said Ten Ha.
"He could have driven us back."
"Yes." said Ten Ha.

She drove back to the highway and began the drive down the winding way to the airport. Ten Ha sat cross-legged in the passenger seat, humming a melodic chant under his breath. Marina snapped her head up suddenly. She realized she had dropped off to sleep for a second. She looked at the cliff and sea far below, just past the guard rail and she shivered. She swung the car around the next bend and saw a car coming towards her in the middle of the road. It was racing fast, half in her lane. A convertible, top down, a young man laughing and looking over at the woman sitting next to him. Marina judged that she had just enough room to swerve a little and squeak between him and the guardrail. But she was too tired and too sore to slip precisely through the narrow gap. The convertible's front fender clipped her car hard. Her car shot through the guard rail and into the air. The front end tipped downward and as she gripped the wheel she saw, with disbelief, the ocean rising up to meet her. The last thing she was aware of as they hit the water, was the sound of Ten Ha droning a deep vibrating sutra chant. She was instantly knocked unconscious, so was unaware of drinking in a deep long breath of water, and never exhaling again. She awoke in darkness, in deep wet, but felt no cold. She floated gently through the roof of the car, seeing herself and Ten Ha, seat belts fastened, bodies slumped forward. For some reason, that seemed comical to her and she smiled as she rose through the water toward a glimmering light. She came gently through the transition of liquid to atmosphere, and continued to float upward toward the now brighter and beckoning light.

She was drawn toward it, faster and faster, until suddenly just an instant before she was subsumed into it, she popped into darkness. Dark, warm, nurturing. She lay curled, flexing, growing ever to the sweet beat of her mother's heart. At first, she remembered all, all whom she had loved. A pleasant sense of Chance, Marina, Buddy, Tara, and Bayou the dog of her childhood; and also moments and places that had enriched her life. She drifted pleasantly, then one day came the squeezing demanding downward journey to the new light. As she came through the birth canal of her mother, all memories vanished from her mind. She blinked in the light of the sun as she felt her mother's tongue roughly cleaning her and rousing her to this new life.

Within a few more days she was romping in her natural element-the Pacific Ocean, just a few short miles from where they had pulled her old discarded body from the wreckage of the drowned car. In her new world, she played with several older seals who had welcomed her with special affection.


In the meantime, during the accident Ten Ha was fully alert as they struck the water: fully aware, calm, and chanting a special sutra for the occasion of accepting death. He never lost consciousness, so he was aware of the second of transition when he no longer needed his flesh and bones. He left them as lightly as he would have left an old suit of clothes on the floor. He floated upward toward the bright light, happy in a sense of release. He entered into the aura of the light and could see a sweet world within. He saw celestial beings wrapped in golden aura, as they floated peacefully in harmony and friendship among a green world of great beauty. Forests, flowers, lakes of heavenly design, a world that showed no suffering. He stopped at the edge of the lighted world and looked back at the darkness from whence he came. There was a choice. He could easily enter into this bright land and live a long lifetime of grace, accruing little or no harm to his purity of soul. Or he could turn back toward the beings left behind; return and continue to alleviate their suffering and help them look for the path of loving one another. He would also have his share in the suffering of that world. With no hesitation, knowing the consequences of his choice, he turned and floated weightlessly down, back towards the darkness.

    He became a spark in the womb of his new mother. He floated in the warm darkness some little time, encompassed in the loving beat. Time came, and he traveled down the tightened tunnel. He emerged. His mother licked away the birth sack from his grey and white fur, he looked up with new and bleary eyes at her white tinged muzzle. She was an old brown stray dog and he was her final puppy. She welcomed him. His childhood passed in slender means but filled with great happiness. He prepared himself for the duties that he had untaken when he made his choice while in the great light.

Chance got the call while he was in the studio with Shep, finishing the sound track. Shep saw the blood drain from his face, he became as grey as a corpse. His voice was suddenly wooden and automatic. "I see." he said tonelessly. "Should I come right away?"

The state trooper on the other end of the line said, "That's up to you, sir. There is really no need as far as we are concerned. If we are able to retrieve the bodies we will need to identify your wife. Do you know if someone else may have been with her? Witnesses reported seeing someone in the passenger seat. "

"Yes, I know who it was. I'll have his people contact you. And now, if you don't mind, I have to hang up. I will call you back in a little while."

He set the receiver carefully back into its cradle, and stared straight ahead. Then he looked down at his hands as if he had never seen them before, he looked randomly around the room. Shep said, "What's up?"

"Marina has had a wreck." Chance answered in a monotone.

"Is she alright? Is she hurt?"

"They think she is dead. The car went over a cliff into the ocean. Ten Ha was probably with her."

Shep stared at him. Both men's minds slipped so far into a hopeless abyss that there were no words for a long minute. Then Shep began to rock and as he clutched the arms of his chair, he chanted, "Oh God, oh God, oh

God...". "Oh God," he said again. "Oh Chance I'm so sorry."

Chance just stared back at him, owl-eyed with disbelief. "She can't be gone. This can't be happening. She can't just be gone. I don't know what to do." He began to smack himself in the head. "What the hell was wrong with me? I let her go. All I had to do was go with her. She would be alive if I had just gone with her. I would have been driving. They say someone was in her lane and she almost made it past them. Oh Shep, I let her go. I wasn't there. She told me she needed me, how could I be so stupid? So blind? She's gone! She's never coming through that door again! Never! Never! Never!"

He began to pace wildly back and forth, frantic, as though if he moved fast enough he could reach out and grab her, pull her back from that moment. He sat down and beat his head with his hands again, tears rolling down his face.

"Stop it! Stop it!" Shep grabbed and held his fists. "Get a hold of yourself, you're going to hurt yourself."

Chance dropped his hands into lap and slumped down, "How can this be happening?" he asked Shep piteously. "Why would this happen to her? She can't be gone."

Shep spoke consoling words, but Chance was beyond listening. All through the night he paced the room, or sat and stared at nothing, mind refusing to grind forward. Neither Shep nor Sylvia could do anything except be present in case he needed them.

In the morning, he fell into an exhausted sleep for a few hours. When he woke, for a short interval he did not remember that Marina was dead. He had this brief lapse of happiness, then reality fell like a wall of bricks and he was swallowed into a heart of darkness.

Police divers pulled Marina's and Ten Ha's bodies from the wreckage. Sylvia and Shep went with Chance on his sad journey to identify her, and see her one more time. When he saw her, she had the same white rubber mask-like look that he had seen with little Danny, when they found his lifeless form at the quarry, so many long years ago. It looked like the sea had made her its own. He touched her hair, matted with salt, only the smell of the sea remained. Even her fragrance was gone. He turned away.

"Where is her necklace?" asked Sylvia. "She never took it off."

The attendant at the morgue looked at the list of effects and said, "There was no necklace, only her wedding ring and her watch." He handed them to Sylvia.

"I guess those charms went back to where ever they came from." said Chance. "Much good did they do her!" he added bitterly.

Marian's body was cremated. Ten Ha was given a Buddhist funeral at a temple in California. The monks in Florida said he had no next of kin to notify, his entire family had died before he left Cambodia.

Chance carried Marina's ashes home to Florida with him. He moved from one breath to the next. Some nights he had the old nightmare visit from Danny, standing dripping in the bedroom doorway, more real than life itself. Staring, never moving, never speaking.

One night, Danny faded and Marina took his place, pale, wet, and dead. Chance leapt from sleep to waking, reaching out to her.

"Oh my girl!" he cried as he tried to hold her in his arms. She was not there. The only moisture on the floor board where he had seen her standing, was the tears he shed as he lay upon the floor.

He moved into the old trailer in Orange Blossom, unable to live in the cottage they had shared.

Sylvia and Shep helped him hold a memorial for Marina and Ten Ha in Orange Blossom. For a few hours the small town was filled with people, all speaking their memories, some comforting, some obtusely hurtful. Chance was made of wood. He shook hands, thanked the mourners for coming, nodded and pretended he was listening. Then he drifted on to the next little cluster of people. The absence was all he could feel.

For six months, Marina's ashes sat on a shelf in the trailer. Chance stopped going to the studio. He spent a lot of time staring at the wall, sometimes he went out to the swamp and sat on the platform where Marina had spent many of her happiest hours. He listened to the birds, thinking it was odd there was still birdsong in the world, when she was not there to hear it. His heart yearned as he tried to make some connection with her, where ever she was. He could find no trace.

One day, as he sat on the platform reaching for her in his mind, he saw a little movement in the water. He focused and saw two ivory colored orbs. Gradually two golden eyes emerged above the waterline, then the nostrils and finally the long white snout. The ruby jewel in the Andeluvian forehead glinted in a ray of sun. Presently, Chance was looking at the huge white alligator as he waded onto the land. He went to the animal, having no concern anymore for his own safety. He stood by the animal's head, and the great upper jaw slowly opened, ivory teeth massive and cruel. Sitting on the bed of the pink fleshy tongue were all the charms from Marina's necklace, even the tiny gold image of Bayou, dog of their childhood.

The animal slowly closed it jaws again, its mouth held that gentle but smug crocodilian smile. The alligator turned slowly and easily, and walked back into the water, gradually sinking out of sight, his grace at odds with his enormous bulk. As he disappeared under the amber brown water, it seemed so final-such a gesture of conclusion that another brittle piece of Chance's heart cracked.

One day, Sylvia, Shep, and Baby May dropped by to visit Chance at the trailer. Tara, the chow dog, was with them. After Tara finished her explosive greeting of Chance, she began to sniff and search around the trailer.

"I think she's looking for Ten Ha." said Chance. Tara came over to him when she heard her master's name, and pushed her head under Chance's hand.

"The monks say she looks for him first thing every morning." Chance patted the head of the dog, thinking how much happiness she had brought to Ten Ha and also to Grace. He wished he had brought a fraction of that to each of them.

"It's not doing you a whole lot of good, being by yourself so much." Sylvia pointed out. "I wish you would come on over and stay with us and Miss Margaret."

"Thanks Sylvia, but I'm not fit company these days."

"That's not the point, Darlin'. We miss them too. I know it's hard for you, but you need to start moving forward a little bit. We're here to help you."

"There's no point." said Chance simply.

"Oh honey, you have your whole life ahead of you."

Chance looked at Baby May sitting on the floor playing with Sylvia's shoelaces. "No, you two have a future ahead of you. I have nothing but the past."

"That's not true; you have us, you have your work."

"I'm in a desert now and I think it's endless. It goes nowhere and it goes on forever. Marina, Grace, Buddy, Ten

Ha- they waited for me to understand and they gave me so much while they waited. And it was all wasted, all their effort. I never got it until they were gone. And now it's too late-they're gone."

"It's going to take time." Shep sought to encourage him.

Chance changed the subject. "I think I'd like to bury Marina's ashes at home with Buddy and Grace. I think she should be resting with them."

A second memorial and funeral were arranged, and they drove with him back to the old hometown, Millertown. Mark and Marie flew down and met them. They stayed at the hotel in town, and the day before the funeral Chance drove himself to Grace's house.

The house had stumbled from neglect. Marina and he had left it empty, and the turning years had taken their toll. The porch sagged, birds flew in and out of a broken window, and the mice had made themselves at home. Chance had the urn of Marina's ashes with him. He sat on the front porch at the head of the steps, urn beside him. He looked down at the straggling garden where Grace and Ten Ha had found so many hours of happiness, working among the flowers. A few tenacious asters and lilies continued to nod among the weeds. It occurred to him that his people had been like the flowers; exquisite- they had the power to evoke such strong feeling in him, he had not seen their fragility; had not sensed how ephemeral they might be. He had looked away and when he turned back, they were gone. He realized the greatest pain in his life came not from the cruel or uncaring people he had met; it was the bite of flowers that cut your heart in two. The bite of gentle flowers not tended, and slipped away. A wave of appreciation washed through him, followed by anguish over all the opportunity lost. Never to go back, with this new found knowledge and be the person they had been waiting for.

He sat on the old porch and saw with a new eye- translucent memories: Marina and Bayou romping under the oak trees; Buddy with a beer in one hand, the other arm wrapped around Grace's waist as they looked out over their world, satisfied with it and their places in it.

He went to meet his friends, and the people of Marina's childhood, in the little graveyard on a wooded knoll above the river. A tiny square hole lay open, to hold the urn. Next to the hole were the tombstones of Buddy and Grace. The minister who spoke had watched Marina grow from childhood, to become the vibrant woman who left their little town and made her mark well on the world. He remembered her caring ways with everyone and every creature. He mentioned Ten Ha, and the gift he brought to their little community, the gift of tenderness and friendship during Grace's long illness and decline. Then he spoke of the sadness of Marina being taken so young, and his faith that it was a loving God who took her home.

Chance was awake to every word. He thanked the minister and shook his hand. "I appreciate you caring." he told him. He was tender with his friends that evening. They all gathered in the suite of Mark and Maria. Conversation was subdued, mostly memories of times with Marina, and also Ten Ha. As the evening was winding down, Chance said to Sylvia, "Do you remember what you said to me when I wouldn't go with Marina to California?"

"Please forgive me for that; I had no idea something like that was going to happen."

"It's alright. You were right."

"No Chance, it wasn't your fault. Accidents just happen sometimes. Please don't do this to yourself anymore."

"It was my fault." he answered quietly. "I should have been there. She told me she needed me and I couldn't hear her. She shouldn't have had to turn to Ten Ha or anybody else. He knew. He went right away when she asked. He knew she wouldn't ask if it wasn't really important. He understood. Well, I do too, now. But you were right when you said that the people who were loving and caring were the source of all I created."

"Yes, but you did the creating. They filled you up, but you are the one who made the deeply beautiful films."

"Shep and I made them. I may have brought my share of the beauty, but any depth came out of Shep. Now I know my people were the stardust, I only breathed it in and molded it into a shape. A pretty shape but not worthy of the stuff that they were made of."

Shep said, "I don't agree with you, but if you feel that way, let's make a movie and see if you can do what you think is right by them. I have a few ideas."

"Everyone in the room raised their glasses, toasting the advent of the next movie project, but Chance kept his glass on the table and said, "Sorry Friend, you're going to have to make it without me. I'm played out. There's no stardust left in my bag. It's been a long day and I think I'll go to bed." His friends watched him sadly as he left the room.

That night he dreamt again of Marina. She stood in his doorway, pale and wet, dripping on the floor. This time he stayed in his bed and spoke quietly to her. He asked her to come to him or give him a sign, some hope of connection with her. She just stood there, no expression on her face. Then she put her hand out to the side and a small pale hand reached out from beyond the doorway and took her hand. Danny stepped into view and stood next to her, just gazing at Chance, no hint of intention in his face. They both dissolved into the darkness. Chance rose slowly and went to feel the floor. Dry as a bone, as always. He went back to bed and tried to summon Marina into his dreams, but she would not come.

He muddled through the winter. With Shep's help, he installed a wood burning stove in the trailer. Then he split enough firewood to keep the chill away in January and February. He was as kind to the people around him as he had always been. He joked some and was more sympathetic than he had been before; but Shep sensed a drifting inside his friend, as if he wasn't well attached to the world anymore.

One day, Shep and Sylvia brought an out-of-town guest to visit him. Marylyn worked in L.A. as a film editor for one of the major movie houses. She was funny, sensitive, attractive, and divorced. Chance was hospitable to her and the afternoon passed pleasantly. The next day, Sylvia came by herself.

"What do you think of my friend?" she asked.

"She seems like a fine woman." said Chance.

"Maybe you should think about dating her while she's in town."

"That holds no interest for me."

"It would do you good."

"You do me good, my friend." He smiled.

"I don't get it. Are you just going to go down like Buddy did?"

"It's not the same thing." he explained patiently. "Buddy saw to the heart of the matter when it came to life. He gave it his all, he helped carry those around him to better ground. He just wore out finally. I think he used up all he had. I wish I was like him."

"Sweetie, it will get better, you've got time."

"I've got plenty of time. I'm just trying to get through it now."

"Honey, there are plenty of other people in this world."

"The people I cared about and cared about me are gone. Marina was the child of my heart. There will be no one else to fill that place. You know, some part of me was missing all that time. I didn't see how much my presence would have comforted Grace. I couldn't look deep enough and see how sick she was. I think I could have eased a lot of Buddy's loneliness on his way out, if I could have understood to reach out to the depths in him. It took losing Marina. And what earthly good does it do to understand, when it's too late? They were waiting for me, I just couldn't get it."

Sylvia was crying softly. "I know you miss her and I know how much you loved her. She knew that, too."

"I hope she did. I think she did." he patted her hand as she dried her tears.

He said, "I want to go to California and go to the place where she died. I couldn't do it when we were there to bring her home, but I'm ready now. I want to stand where she was last on this earth. It's the last thing I can think to do, to try and touch some part of her."

He went the next week, wanting to be there for the anniversary of her death. Friends offered to go with him, but he wanted to go by himself. He stayed in the hotel room where she had stayed. Sat looking out over the blue ocean that had swallowed her. It looked so endlessly immense as it stretched unruffled to the horizon. He wondered how he could ever reach out through it to find her spirit somewhere in all that watery space. He watched the sun dip into the ocean and thought of her watching that same sun go down for the last time.

    The next day he drove the winding coastal highway along the curves, high above the surging waves that breathed in a pulse against the rock cliffs. He drove to the spot where she had gone over; the new guardrail was still shiny where it had been replaced. He parked at a nearby overlook and walked back, then stood on the narrow band of grass between the road and the rail. He imagined in his mind's eye, the car in its soaring trajectory, then its plunging entry into the water below. He wondered what Marina was thinking as she dove to her death. He thought she was probably not afraid. He looked down hoping to see dolphins, although he didn't know if it was a place where it was likely they would be. He just wanted to see them so he could imagine that two of them were the ones Marina set free. Imagine they were telling him how grateful they were for the last and final act of her life. He saw no dolphins. He was surprised how disappointed he was; thinking that they would have appeared for Marina. He took it as just more proof that he was unworthy of anymore magic in his life. He took a last look, then went back to the car.

    He drove north reaching San Francisco in the late afternoon. At random, he chose an old hotel: multi-storied, anonymously dreary. His was a room on a middle floor with a grey view of another sad old brick building across a grimy courtyard. He lay down on the bed and dropped into sleep.

    In the morning he got up still fully clothed and was surprised he had no memory of dreaming. Just before sunrise he drove slowly through deserted streets damp with the residue of the night's fog. Although the sky was heavy and dark, the streets reflected a diffused pink light from the as yet, unseen sun. He rolled slowly through the park that led to the Golden Gate Bridge, rounded gentle curves enclosing un-peopled greens of dew-filled grass.

    At the entrance to the bridge, he left his car. He looked back at the city shining now in the first light, then he turned and walked out onto the footpath of the browning reddish orange bridge. The metal was dripping as the fog pulled back its fingers, retreating out over to sea. He walked with an even pace, unhurried but with some destination in mind. As he walked, more and more of the bay water appeared from beneath the fog. By the time he reached the midpoint he could see clearly out to the horizon line.

    He climbed easily up onto the rail. He stood there evenly balanced. The water below looked cold, unwelcoming and lay far beneath him. There was a platinum sheen on the fractured reflective surface. He raised his head, looking outward. Then he stepped out of his insupportable present into the unsupported air. He fell like a spear downward toward the cold cold water below. He fell so fast his only thoughts were of the physical; the sensation of speed and gathering velocity, his body rushing downward to meet the embrace of gravity. Wind roared in his ears, the horizon rushed upward past him, and then he hit. He reflexively pointed his toes, and his arms shot up above his head just before impact. He sliced in cleanly, hardly slowed by the weight of the water he was plummeting through, on his downward journey to the bottom of the bay. As the water rushed past him, he had a sudden recall of plunging off a cliff, leaping with no fear, trying to save Danny. He had been frantically searching for life in the deep dark waters of the quarry. Today he was moving faster, deeper. This time he knew he was seeking the dead. He blacked out in the inky depth.

He awoke in darkness, in deep wet. He felt a tremendous pressure in his chest as he was being pushed upward toward a glimmering light. He was rising rapidly, being pushed by forces beneath him. As he neared the brightening light, he had a growing sense of desperate urgency. His head burst above the water and every fibre of awareness in him participated in drawing in a huge gulping breath. He drew another breath that seemed as deep as the bay beneath him, and then, uncontrollably, a primal cheer of exaltation ripped out of him, singing across the water, every cell shouting out the joy of simply being alive.

He was supported, head kept above water by the same mysterious force that had propelled him to the surface. He panicked briefly when he realized he was surrounded by animals as big as himself, black shapes moving purposefully around him. Were they sharks? Then he realized it was those very animals who were keeping him afloat. They were seals! Not only had they brought him up, they were now industriously shoving him crosswise, cutting diagonally against a fierce rip current that was trying to sweep him out to sea. Sometimes a round shiny face popped up and looked at him or at the shore, but mostly their attention was focused on the enormous effort of struggling his weight forward while keeping his head above water. He tried to help in his own rescue, but found his arms and legs were numb with cold and useless to him. He gave himself over to their control. The shore was approaching, there was a little beach. As the current subsided, the seals kept their heads above water for longer spells, and looked at him with great tenderness from beautiful black liquid eyes. He thought they looked like the eyes of animistic angels.

A smaller seal swam up to him and he could see something was wrapped around its neck. He was going to try and free her from whatever it was, when she reared up high enough for him to see that it was Marina's necklace, and all the charms were hanging from it, even the dog that he had given to his girl. He reached out but the seal slid below the surface. He saw the gold glimmering briefly as she disappeared in the opaque water. He passed out from the cold.

He came to lying on the little beach; half in, half out of the water. He shivered hard and somehow clawed his way a little farther until he was completely out of the water.

He lay on the gritty pebbles, his teeth chattered and he shook uncontrollably, numb with cold. He was able to raise his head a little and as he looked forward he saw a young boy straddling a bicycle. Next to him sat a grey and white dog. The boy came down from the road, his dog at his heels. Chance's head fell back down to the gravel.

He felt a small hand shaking him by the shoulder, "Mister! Mister! Are you alright?"

Chance rolled onto his side facing him. Through his clattering teeth he said, "I think I am. I sure am cold."

The boy helped him to a sitting position as Chance continued shivering in an alarming fashion.

The child said, "Put your arms around Prince. He can keep you warm while I go get a blanket. I'll be right back." He ran off toward a set of ramshackle Victorian houses that lined the pot-holed beach road. The dog sat obediently close to Chance and leaned up against him. Chance hugged the dog as well as he could with his almost lifeless arms.

The warmth from the dog began to seep into Chance's body. He looked up as he heard the scrunching of the boy's sneakers. He carried a torn and stained quilt, which he draped around man and dog.

"Is that better?" he asked.

"Much better." replied Chance gratefully through thawing lips.

I can't let you keep it." the boy said regretfully. "My mom will whip me if she finds out I took my covers outside."

Chance hastily tried to unwrap it saying, "We don't want that to happen. Why don't you take it back right now!"

"No, that's okay." answered the boy. "She's still sleeping and so is the guy she brought home. She won't get up til this afternoon, she's on the late shift today."

The feeling was returning to Chance's hands, he wiggled them in the thick ruff of the dog's neck. He felt a collar and traced along it casually until his fingers encountered an odd-feeling tag. He clumsily parted the thick fur and bent his head to look more closely. There hung the golden dog charm.

"Where did you get this?" he asked a little too abruptly.

The boy answered defensively, "He had it on him when he came."

"Where did he come from?" Chance asked more gently.

"I don't know. He followed me home one day." Then the boy said fiercely, "He's mine! He wants to be with me!"

Chance looked more closely at Prince and found himself looking into a pair of familiar brown eyes- serene, trustworthy and wise. A warm smile gradually spread across Chance's face as a few tears fell like slowly falling stars. They splashed one by one onto the dog's fur. He said, "I know he belongs with you."

The boy was relieved. "Mom makes him sleep outside. Even when it's cold. But she's gone a lot, so I sneak him in and he sleeps with me." The boy was sitting on the other side of Chance. He picked something up from the sand.

"Are these yours?" he asked. In his hand was a group of charms: two golden dolphins, a silver bear with three little marks on its leg, a white alligator with a tiny red jewel in its forehead, and three golden little seals. The smallest seal had a minute fairy-sized little necklace with gold charms so tiny they were not discernable to the naked eye. As Chance gazed at them mutely, the boy asked him again, "Are these yours?"

"Yes," said Chance, "I reckon they are." He wrapped them carefully in his damp handkerchief and slipped them into his pocket. He stood up, feeling better now. The boy and dog stood alongside him as he looked out over the bay.

The boy asked, "What were you doing out there? Were you playing with the seals?"

The man looked down at the boy, put his hand on his shoulder, shrugged, and then said, "You know, it's not that interesting. What have you been doing today?"

Made in the USA
Charleston, SC
14 March 2016